Mills & Boon Classics

A chance to read and collect some of the best-loved novels from Mills & Boon — the world's largest publisher of romantic fiction.

Every month, four titles by favourite Mills & Boon authors will be re-published in the *Classics* series.

A list of other titles in the *Classics* series can be found at the end of this book.

Anne Mather

WHITE ROSE OF WINTER

MILLS & BOON LIMITED
LONDON · TORONTO

All the characters in this book have no existence outside the imagination of the Author, and have no relation whatsoever to anyone bearing the same name or names. They are not even distantly inspired by any individual known or unknown to the Author, and all the incidents are pure invention.

The text of this publication or any part thereof may not be reproduced or transmitted in any form or by any means, electronic or mechanical, including photocopying, recording, storage in an information retrieval system, or otherwise, without the written permission of the publisher.

This book is sold subject to the condition that it shall not, by way of trade or otherwise, be lent, resold, hired out or otherwise circulated without the prior consent of the publisher in any form of binding or cover other than that in which it is published and without a similar condition including this condition being imposed on the subsequent purchaser.

First Published 1973
This edition 1980

© Anne Mather 1973

Australian copyright 1980
Philippine copyright 1980

ISBN 0 263 73256 8

Set in 10 on 11½pt Plantin

*Made and printed in Great Britain by
C. Nicholls & Company Ltd
The Philips Park Press, Manchester*

CHAPTER ONE

LONDON AIRPORT seemed drab and miserable after the colour and vitality of Kuala Lumpur, its illuminated buildings sheltering in a mist of fine rain. There were no exotically patterned *cheongsams* here, not even the tantalizing glimpse of a *songbok* among the throng of people bustling towards waiting relatives and friends. It was as cold and alien as Malaysia had seemed six years before, thought Julie unhappily, hunching her slim shoulders beneath the soft sable coat which she had bought on Barbara's advice for the homeward journey.

And yet London no longer looked like home. Home was a single-storied dwelling on the shores of the South China Sea, and although when she had first seen it she had thought she was going to hate living there, hate everything about her new life, in fact, time and affection had served to make it the reality and her life in London merely the hopefully forgotten past.

But now she was back in England again, and somehow she had to accept that the bungalow outside of Rhatoon was no longer the refuge it had become. It was up to her to adapt to her changed circumstances quickly so that Emma should not find it all too painful.

An attractive stewardess was urging her passengers forward towards the Customs and clearance buildings, smiling as she bade some of them farewell, saving a particularly warm expression for the small girl holding Julie's hand.

'Good-bye, Emma,' she said, bending down to take her hand. 'And thank you for your assistance during the flight. I don't know how we should have managed without you.'

Emma glanced mischievously up at Julie, her grey eyes

dancing. Then she looked back at the stewardess. 'Did I really help? Mummy said I was probably more nuisance than I was worth.'

The stewardess's smile widened. 'On the contrary. Who else would have handed out all those magazines, if you hadn't been around?'

Julie's lips turned up at the corners. 'It was kind of you to let her help,' she said. 'It made the journey so much less arduous for her.'

The stewardess made a deprecatory gesture. 'That's all right, Mrs. Pemberton. We enjoyed her company.'

'Well, thank you again.' Julie bit her lip. 'Say good-bye now, darling. We shan't be seeing Miss Forrest again.'

'G'bye, Miss Forrest,' responded Emma politely, and Julie smiled before walking on.

The stewardess had been kind, but then most people were kind to Emma. She was one of those children that attracted attention wherever she went. It wasn't that she was a particularly rosy-cheeked individual; on the contrary, her skin was pale and did not respond to sunlight, and her hair was black and completely straight, yet for all that she possessed that certain something that singled her out from the ordinary. In the beginning, this knowledge had caused Julie no little anxiety, but as time went by she realized it was simply a family resemblance and not something that belonged exclusively to Emma's father.

Their luggage was being cleared, their passports checked; everyone was so friendly and polite to the attractive young woman who was travelling with only her five-year-old daughter as companion. But beyond the glass partitioning a throng of people were waiting impatiently and Julie hugged her coat closer about her suddenly, feeling cold and apprehensive. She avoided looking in that direction. Somehow she wanted to delay the moment when she must take up contact again with Michael's family, and only when Emma tugged her hand and demanded excitedly: 'Where's Grandma? Can you see her, Mummy?' did she cast a cursory glance towards the reception lounge.

'Not yet, darling,' she murmured faintly, glancing round to ascertain that their cases were all together. Most of their heavier luggage had gone by sea, in trunks, but they had a couple of cases with them containing necessary changes of clothing.

'But you did say that Grandma was coming to meet us, didn't you, Mummy?' Emma asked persistently. 'I 'spect she's waiting with those other people, don't you?'

'I expect so, darling.' Julie heaved a deep breath. 'Come along. We'll go and see.'

Disdaining the use of a porter, Julie picked up a case in each hand and directing Emma to carry her airline bag they emerged into the reception area. Lucy Pemberton, Michael's mother, had said she would meet them at the airport, but she was notoriously unreliable and Julie was not surprised to find no sign of her. She sighed. Were she not feeling so hollow already. Lucy's non-appearance to meet the daughter-in-law she had not seen for almost six years might have aroused a distinctly unpleasant ache in the region of her heart, but the events of the past three months had been so traumatic anyway, she felt almost empty of emotion.

Only Emma's small face drooped with disappointment. 'She's not here!' she announced indignantly. 'Oh, Mummy, why? Why isn't she here like she said she would be?'

Julie bent to the child, putting down the cases with a sigh. 'Don't upset yourself, darling. Grandma is probably on her way at this very moment. But you don't know what it's like here. The traffic is very busy! And she's most likely been caught in a traffic jam. You know what they are now, don't you?'

Emma sniffed. 'I s'pose so. But why didn't she set out

quickly enough to be here to meet us?' Emma was a very logical child.

Julie shook her head, straightening. 'I don't know, darling.' She glanced surreptitiously at the broad masculine watch on her slim wrist. The plane had landed only a few minutes behind schedule. Lucy *should* have been here. 'How would you like to go into the restaurant and have a Coke?' she suggested. 'Just until Grandma arrives? In fact I could see if I could telephone her from the restaurant.'

Emma frowned. 'Won't we miss her, though? I mean – if she arrives just after we've gone into the restaurant?'

Julie sighed again. 'No. Look, if we sit near the windows we'll be able to see everyone coming and going.'

Emma was unconvinced and Julie felt impatient suddenly. It should not have been too much to ask that Lucy should be here on time just this once. Particularly after the thousands of miles they had travelled. Didn't she realize that after such a flight one was tired and disorientated, unable to cope with the usual upsets with the same degree of calmness?

A thought struck her. What if Lucy had forgotten altogether? It was not impossible. If it was her bridge afternoon, or her golf afternoon; (did people play golf in the rain?) or even one of those charity whist drives she loved to organize, it was quite possible that their arrival should pass unnoticed.

And after all, she had never liked Julie. She had shown that quite plainly. The very last thing she had wanted was for her to marry one of her beloved sons, and when that happened Michael had made things easier by taking the appointment in Rhatoon.

There was always Emma, of course. Three years ago when Michael had brought the child to England, he had said that his mother had doted on the child, but perhaps things would be different now that Julie was here. And Michael was dead...

'Well, we can't stay here,' Julie said now, trying to sound competent and reasonable. 'Come along, darling. I could do with a cup of tea myself.'

'Julie!'

The hard masculine tones brought Julie up short and she turned reluctantly to face the man who had spoken. Even before she turned she knew exactly who it was, and her nerves jerked with exhaustion. Now was not the moment to confront Robert Pemberton, not when she was tired and uneasy and absurdly vulnerable, even after all this time.

Tall and lean, with hair as dark and straight as Emma's brushing the collar of his expensively casual cream suede suit, he looked sleek and powerful, and compellingly sure of himself. He was not a handsome man, neither of the Pembertons had been that, but like Emma he possessed that elusive element of charm, and consequently he had always made other men, more strictly handsome men, seem insipid by comparison. He did not seem to have changed at all, except perhaps that his eyes were more deeply set in a face that wore a year-round tan due to the countless trips abroad he was able to make, and his expression did nothing to aid her failing confidence. Indeed, if anything he was regarding her with faint contempt and his lips twisted wryly as she held out a rather unsteady hand.

'Hello, Robert,' she managed. 'How are you?'

He shook her hand briefly, his own cool and detached, his gaze flickering over her with painful appraisal. He had always had the knack of being able to reduce her to embarrassment by the directness of his stare, but on this occasion she endeavoured to hide her confusion, forcing herself to the knowledge that she was no longer a girl, no longer in his employ; she was a woman who had been married and widowed, with a five-year-old daughter. She must not think of all that had gone before. That was in the past. She must live for the present and think only of the future. Emma's future.

Now Robert dropped her hand and said coolly, 'I'm fine, thank you. And you?' It was a formality, nothing more.

'Fine. Fine.' Julie assumed a mask of composure, hiding behind it like a fugitive fleeing from justice. Whenever she was emotionally disturbed she tried to do this, knowing that to an outsider she must appear cold and indifferent when this definitely was not the case.

Robert regarded her broodingly for a long moment, and she thought he was about to mention Michael, but then he dropped to his haunches beside the child. 'Hello, Emma,' he said. 'Remember me?'

Emma stared at him consideringly. 'No – o,' she replied honestly. 'But you look a little bit like Daddy, so I s'pose you must be Uncle Robert.'

'That's right.' Robert smiled, the coldness which had been evident in his manner when he was speaking to Julie disappearing beneath Emma's innocent charm. 'Who told you I looked like Daddy?'

'Mummy told me.' Emma glanced up at Julie for a moment. 'Didn't you?'

Julie made an involuntary gesture, but Robert's eyes never left the child's face. 'I see. And do I rate a kiss?'

Emma hesitated. 'All right,' she agreed, and leaning forward touched his cheek with her soft lips. She wrinkled her nose when it was over. 'But why were you so late? And where's Grandma? Mummy said she was coming to meet us. Where is she?'

Robert straightened, and looking round beckoned a porter to come and take their cases. Then he looked down and said: 'Grandma couldn't come. She's not feeling well.'

Julie glanced at him quickly, sensing a rebuke, but he was not looking at her. He was talking to the porter, indicating the luggage, pointing outside to where his car was waiting.

He had the supreme self-confidence that comes from always being used to giving orders, and Julie felt a fleeting irritation that he should so arrogantly take charge of the situation without offering any explanations, without even telling her where his mother was or why she should not be feeling well.

Now he turned. 'Let's go,' he said, to no one in particular. 'My car's this way. We can talk on the way to town.'

Emma slipped her hand into Julie's again, drawing her mother's attention to herself. 'Is it all right?' she whispered. Emma's whispers were all of the stage variety, and Robert could not fail to have heard her.

'I expect so,' replied Julie, managing a slight smile. 'Come on. We'll soon be able to have a bath and change our clothes. And those eyes look very tired, young lady.'

Emma smiled. 'It's exciting, though, isn't it?' she breathed. 'I mean – we are here, aren't we? In London. Do you think Grandma will be better by tomorrow?'

Julie shook her head. 'I have no idea,' she answered shortly, and was conscious of a faint reaction from the man ahead of them. He seemed to hesitate, as though he was about to say something more, but then he went on, his broad shoulders blocking Julie's vision until they reached the swing doors and he stood aside politely to allow her to precede him.

Robert's car was a pale grey Aston Martin, sleek and powerful, like the man himself. Six years ago, Julie reflected, he had driven an E-type Jaguar, but perhaps his tastes had changed since then. The porter stowed their cases in the boot of the car, and straightened to thank Robert enthusiastically for the tip he received. Robert seemed indifferent to the man's gratitude, his face expressionless as he held open the passenger door for Julie to get in. Emma clambered into the back, bouncing up and down on the seat.

'Isn't it a super car?' she exclaimed, her annoyance at the non-appearance of her grandmother vanishing in the excitement of the moment.

'Super,' echoed Julie, a trifle dryly, giving her small daughter a smile before hunching her shoulders in the soft fur coat.

Robert came to get in beside her, slamming his door and flicking the ignition with impatient precision. His thigh was only a few inches away from hers, and she had only to move her leg slightly to encounter his, and the realization brought back a flood of recollections she had forced herself to believe were forgotten. But was anything truly forgotten? she asked herself. Was it not more accurate to say that the mind could shed veils over things one wanted to forget, and until those veils were torn aside one could delude oneself into believing anything?

Robert turned on the screen wipers as they moved out of the parking area into the stream of traffic making for the city. The rain wasn't heavy, but it was grey and dismal, causing the cars to use their lights even though it was only the middle of the afternoon. To Emma, it was all curiously new and exciting, but Julie shivered. She knew how cold and miserable London could seem in November.

Robert was an expert driver, his long-fingered hands sliding smoothly round the wheel, his eyes intent on the road ahead. However, as the traffic thinned on the motorway, he said: 'There are some cigarettes in the glove compartment, if you'd like one.'

Julie shook her head. 'I seldom smoke,' she replied politely. Then, for Emma's sake, she went on: 'I hope your mother's not seriously ill.'

Robert flicked a glance in her direction. 'A cold, nothing more.'

'I see,' Julie linked her fingers together in her lap.

'Where are you taking us, Uncle Robert?' Emma asked,

her arms resting on the backs of their seats. It was the question Julie had wanted to ask since Robert met them at the airport, but had been unable to voice.

Robert swung past a lumbering wagon before replying. Then he said casually: 'We're going into the city, Emma. I live there. I have an apartment. Would you like to see it?'

Julie looked swiftly at him. 'Where's your mother?'

Robert's expression hardened. 'Don't alarm yourself, Julie. She'll be there waiting for us.'

'I'm not alarmed!' Julie couldn't prevent the sharpness of the retort. She hated this feeling of tension he was deliberately creating, and although Emma could not be aware of it, she resented it.

'You mean Grandma is waiting for us at your apartment?' cried Emma excitedly.

'That's right. She's longing to see you again.'

Robert's tone was entirely different when he spoke to Emma. And well it might be, thought Julie dryly. After all, she could hardly expect Robert to welcome her warmly after everything that had happened. But perhaps outright anger would have been better to cope with than this curt civility that was so chilling, so cold-blooded...

'Your mother lives with you, then?' Julie ventured at last. She *had* to ask.

Robert shook his head. 'No. She doesn't live in Richmond any more, as you possibly know, but she has an apartment of her own in town.'

'I see.' Julie frowned. She didn't altogether care for that. If they were to live with Lucy, as she had led them to believe from her letters, an apartment in town was not the environment Julie would have chosen for Emma. After the freedom of the last few years it would be very hard for her to adapt.

And Robert was making things no easier by behaving as though she should be content to wait and see what was to happen to them. And he still hadn't mentioned Michael! Why? Because of Emma's presence? Or for some other reason? Surely he must realize after three months that they were both able to accept the situation, however distressing it might be. But it was not up to her to bring up that subject, so she said nothing.

'Will I be able to see Buckingham Palace from my window?' Emma was asking now, and Julie turned to reprove her with gentle tolerance. 'London's not like Rhatoon, darling,' she said, smiling. 'There are lots and lots of buildings here. Skyscrapers, too. You know what they are, don't you?'

Emma's lips drooped. 'What will we see, then? The sea?'

Julie sighed. 'No, not the sea. Probably more houses,' she added dryly.

Robert changed down rapidly. 'Stop trying to put the child off even before she's seen where she's going to live,' he said briefly. Then, to Emma: 'Actually, you can see Buckingham Palace from the apartment windows.'

Julie's cheeks burned at the reproof, but Emma was delighted. 'Can you? Can you really? Is it very high up?'

'Very high up,' agreed Robert. 'The top of a skyscraper, in fact.'

'Gosh!' Emma was impressed. 'How do we get up there? Are there lots of stairs? Do we go round and round like we did in the pagoda—'

'There are lifts,' inserted Julie shortly, trying to calm her indignation. She realized her explanations to Emma must have sounded off-putting, but she was tired, too. Couldn't Robert make allowances for that?

'Electric lifts,' said Robert, continuing his conversation with Emma almost as though Julie was not present. 'You work them yourself. You just press a button for the floor you want, and up you go.'

'But what if the lift's upstairs and you're downstairs?' asked Emma, with her painstaking logic.

Robert grinned at her over his shoulder, but Julie looked away. She couldn't bear the realization that unless she was careful Robert would succeed in winning Emma's affection. She didn't want that. It might be a selfish thought, but that was something she could not accept. Not now. Not now that Michael was dead.

Oh, why had he had to die? she asked herself for the umpteenth time. Their world had seemed so peaceful, so secure. And now it was shattered.

Neither Robert nor Emma were aware of her anxieties. 'Good question,' Robert was remarking in answer to Emma's query. 'Well, you press another button, and the lift automatically comes down to you. And in the same way, if you're upstairs and the lift is down it comes up. Of course, it's an enormous building, so there are six lifts really.'

Emma was impressed. 'But what would you do if the lifts broke down?' she asked. 'If there was no electricity to work them.'

Robert slowed behind a stream of cars entering Hammersmith flyover. 'There are stairs to use in an emergency,' he answered. 'But I shouldn't care to have to climb them, would you? Those short legs of yours might wear away before you reached the top.'

Emma giggled, and Julie steeled herself to look about her with feigned interest. But in actual fact, it was interesting. So much old building had gone and in its place the concrete structures of streamlined living. The motorways were a revelation, linking and interlinking in a network of steel girders. She wondered whether she would ever dare drive here again after the quiet roads around Rhatoon, and then decided rather wryly that she might not get the chance. After all, Michael had left all his shares in the company to the family, and what little income she had in her own right would scarcely run to a car. Indeed, she expected to have to return to secretarial work to support herself. She didn't want to feel beholden to the Pembertons.

By the time they reached Sloane Street and turned into Eaton Gate, Julie had her bearings again. Inner London had changed much less than the outskirts, and it was all painfully familiar. They passed the end of the street where the Pemberton Construction Company had its offices, and she recalled with clarity her first day there in the typing pool. She had been very young in those days, and it wasn't until later that she progressed up the scale to become Vincent Harvey's secretary, and through him had been introduced to the chairman, Robert Pemberton. Her nerves tautened. The classic situation, she thought bitterly. Ideal scope for the romantic. But how disastrously it had all ended.

Robert was turning into a quiet square and presently he brought the car to a halt in the forecourt of an immense block of apartments. Even in the rain, Julie could see how impressive it all was, the sculptured forecourt with its formal gardens and fountains, the shallow steps leading up to a row of swing glass doors, the commissionaire from his office vetting all would-be visitors. Recognizing Robert's car, he saluted politely and Robert raised a casual hand in his direction as he slid from behind the wheel.

When Robert opened the boot to take out their luggage, the commissionaire left his office to approach them. 'Good afternoon, sir. May I be of assistance?'

Robert shook his head, drops of water sparkling on the thick darkness of his hair. 'Thank you, Norris, I can manage. Miserable afternoon, isn't it?'

'Yes, sir.' Norris looked curiously at Julie and Emma, who had climbed out of the car and were standing together looking vaguely lost and alien.

Robert intercepted Norris's interest and standing down the cases, he straightened and slammed the boot lid. 'My sister-in-law and her daughter are staying with me for a few days,' he commented by way of an explanation. 'They've just arrived back from Malaya.'

Julie's eyes widened at this unexpected piece of information. They were to stay with *Robert*?

But she could not say anything with Norris looking on, so she confined herself to a pointed stare at her brother-in-law. However, Robert seemed utterly indifferent to her reaction, and picking up the cases he indicated that they should precede him into the building.

Julie took Emma's hand and climbed the shallow steps seething with indignation. What did he mean? Why were they to stay with him? Lucy had said in her letters that they were to stay with her, that she was lonely now that Robert had his own apartment, that she would welcome them into her home wholeheartedly. Needless to say, Julie had taken this with some degree of scepticism. She knew her mother-in-law too well to believe that she should have changed her attitude towards her. But even so, she had never doubted the truth of the arrangements.

In the cramped environs of the lift, cramped with two adults, one child, and two suitcases, Julie had to say something.

'Why are we to stay with you, Robert? I understood from your mother's letters we were to stay with her.'

Robert was propped indolently against the wall of the lift, his legs astride the cases. 'Now now, Julie,' he responded curtly. Then to the child: 'Well, Emma? What do you think?'

Emma was thankfully too young to be aware of the undercurrents present in the adults' conversation and smiled up at him. 'Does it take very long to reach the top?'

'Not very. We'll be there in a few seconds. Look – can you see the red light moving behind those numbers? They're the numbers of the floors we're passing. See – ours is this one, right at the top.'

Emma's eyes grew wide. 'Oh, yes. Look, Mummy, we're almost there. Gosh, my tummy feels all empty somehow.'

There was a slowing moment when Emma looked slightly disconcerted at the sudden change in her metabolism, and then the lift stopped and Robert opened the door.

They stepped out on to a pile-carpeted hallway, but although all the lifts opened on to this hall there were only two doors, and one of them was obviously a service door. Julie was impressed in spite of herself. Robert's apartment must be huge.

Robert lifted the cases, but as they reached the door into the apartment it opened and a man, dressed all in black, stood waiting for them. He was middle-aged, with greying gingery hair, and a ginger moustache.

'Oh, hello there, sir,' he greeted Robert cheerfully, his round face beaming. 'I heard the lift and I said to Mrs. Pemberton, I bet that's Mr. Robert, and it is!'

Robert smiled faintly. 'Very efficient,' he remarked dryly. 'Here, you can take these cases.'

'Yes, sir.'

The man came forward and as he did so Robert glanced rather reluctantly at Julie. Then he said shortly: 'This is Halbird, Julie. He goes everywhere with me. He's a sort of general factotum, I suppose. At any rate, he's capable of turning his hand to anything.'

Julie smiled the sort of wintry smile that was all her tight features would run to. 'Good afternoon, Halbird.'

'Good afternoon, madam. And you, too, miss,' he added, looking warmly at Emma. 'I hope you had a pleasant journey. Not much of a day for arriving back here, though, is it? Miserable!'

'Miserable,' echoed Julie, and Emma, with her usual curiosity, said:

'Why hasn't your moustache gone grey, like your hair?'

'Emma!' Julie was horrified, but both Halbird and Robert

laughed.

'I don't know, little missy,' he replied, picking up the cases. 'Perhaps the frost hasn't penetrated that far yet.'

'What do you mean?' Emma frowned.

'You can discuss the merits of Halbird's appearance later, young woman,' observed Robert then. 'Come along. Grandma's waiting to see you.'

But not to the extent of coming to the door to greet them, thought Julie bitterly, and then chided herself for being so petty. She had been in the country scarcely more than an hour and already she was allowing the situation to upset her.

'Do go in,' Robert directed, his voice noticeably cooler as he addressed his sister-in-law, but Julie drew back.

'You lead the way, Robert,' she insisted. 'After all, it is your apartment.'

Robert's eyes were hard as they encountered her defensive green ones for a brief moment, and then without a word he took Emma by the hand and walked through the cream panelled door. Julie followed more slowly, her heels sinking into the soft carpet of the entrance hall. The tapestry-hung walls were highlighted by examples of native wood-carving he had collected on his various trips abroad, and there was a cedar wood chest on which stood a vase of Peking jade which Julie realized must be priceless.

Robert didn't stop to give them time to remove their coats but opened the door into the lounge beyond, ushering Emma before him. Julie heard her mother-in-law's exclamation of delight when she saw her granddaughter, and then she, too, entered the huge room. And it was huge, stretching as it did from one side of the apartment block to the other, the outer wall a miracle of plate glass. But before Julie could take in the exquisite appointments of it all, her eyes focused on the woman reclining gracefully on a low couch near the windows, presently embracing Emma, and exclaiming at how tall she was and how grown-up she seemed from the toddler she remembered.

Julie stood hesitantly on the thick apricot-coloured carpet, feeling ridiculously youthful and vulnerable as she had always done in this woman's presence. She could remember clearly the first time she had been introduced to Lucy Pemberton. Robert had introduced them, and she had known from the outset that no girl would ever live up to the standards Lucy Pemberton expected for her sons.

But now Lucy seemed to remember her daughter-in-law, and holding Emma close to her with one arm, she extended a hand to Julie. 'Julie darling,' she exclaimed. 'Forgive me! But it's so enchanting to see Emma again, and after – after everything that's happened...'

Julie responded immediately to the emotion in Lucy's voice, hurrying forward to bend and kiss her mother-in-law's perfumed cheek. 'It's good to see you again, too, Lucy,' she averred warmly, and then realized that Lucy hadn't exactly said it was good to see *her*. But she thrust such uncharitable thoughts aside and when Lucy patted the couch beside her, she subsided into the seat and loosened her coat with nervous fingers.

'I must apologize for not being at the airport to meet you,' Lucy went on, her expression indulgent. 'But I've had the most dreadful cold, and Robert insisted I stay here.'

'That's all right.' Julie was quick to deny that any offence had been taken. 'And are you feeling better?'

'Oh, much better.' Lucy looked up at Robert, who was standing watching this interchange rather grimly. 'Darling, do you think Halbird could provide us with some tea? I'm sure Julie would love a cup, wouldn't you, dear?'

Julie nodded, avoiding Robert's critical stare. 'Thank you, that would be lovely.'

'Oh, there's so much to say!' exclaimed Lucy suddenly, hugging Emma close to her. 'You and I have got to get to know one another properly, haven't we, Emma?'

Halbird had carried in the cases and disappeared with them through another door which obviously led to the other rooms of the apartment, and Robert departed, obviously in search of him.

'Do you live here, Grandma?' Emma asked, looking about her in wonder, and Julie was not surprised. Life in Rhatoon had hardly prepared her for such apparent luxury. Apart from its size, the lounge was extensively furnished, but despite the quality of the furnishings it was not a bleak room. There was a warmth about it, a lived-in quality, that appealed to Julie in spite of herself. Even so, to a little girl it was all rather overwhelming and Emma seemed fascinated by the pseudo cowl-fire which broke up the central area and provided a focal point.

'No, darling,' Lucy was replying now. 'Nowhere so grand. I have a flat in a mews not far from here. You'll see it in good time, I expect. But Uncle Robert uses his apartment for entertaining, so naturally it has to be very grand and important.'

'Entertaining?' repeated Emma. 'You mean he puts on shows?'

Lucy chuckled, and Julie felt impatient suddenly. Surely someone should tell *her* what was going on. Why were they here? Why weren't they staying with Lucy as arranged. And why didn't Lucy say something? When were they all going to talk? Really talk, about the things that really mattered! Like Michael's death, for example!

CHAPTER TWO

EMMA was asleep, and Julie was changing for dinner.

The afternoon tea Halbird had provided, a delicious spread of wafer-thin sandwiches, savoury biscuits, and cream cakes, had been more than enough to make Emma drowsy, and after a swift shower she had tumbled into bed without any protest.

Their rooms were linked by the bathroom, which they were to share, and as with the lounge the appointments were attractively exquisite. Emma's bedroom was smaller than her mother's with a fluffy blue carpet and pale blue curtains and covers, while Julie's room had a white carpet and violet covers and curtains. Both rooms had long fitted units to take their clothes, and during tea Halbird had hung those garments which were likely to crease in the wardrobes. The trunks containing the rest of their belongings had not arrived yet, but Julie expected they would be here in a few days as they had been sent in advance.

Julie surveyed her reflection critically in the dressing-table mirror as she brushed her hair. Had she changed much? Could Robert see much difference in her? Did she look much older?

She sighed. What did it matter what Robert thought? Although nothing had been said yet about the change in arrangements she knew that if they were to stay here for a few days it must be that Lucy had not been entirely truthful when it came to explaining the circumstances. And Julie had no intention of remaining in Robert's apartment any longer than was absolutely necessary. Even if it meant taking a job and finding a flat of their own.

She leant forward to examine the shadows beneath her

eyes. She was not sleeping well, and it was beginning to show. She pressed her lips together impatiently. What did it matter? There was no one to care how she looked here, of that she had few doubts. Lucy was accepting her because of Emma, and Robert...

A sliver of apprehension caused an involuntary shudder. She would not think of the past. She would think only of the present. And to hell with the rest.

She rose from the dressing-table stool and smoothed the skirt of the one and only evening dress she had carried with her, a slim-fitting gown of dark blue crepe jersey, that brushed her ankles and accentuated her excessive fairness and slenderness of figure. Her hair she wore as she always wore it, straight as a silver curtain about her shoulders.

When she was satisfied that there was no improvement she could make she emerged from her room and walked slowly along the panelled hall to the double doors of the lounge. A faint odour of continental coffee pervaded the air, and she sniffed appreciatively. She was not hungry, she had eaten little of Halbird's spread at teatime, but she did enjoy good coffee.

Lamps illuminated the lounge, giving a curiously intimate atmosphere to a room that could never be described as such. And yet it was warm and comfortable, and deserted at the moment.

Julie closed the doors behind her and walked across to the plate glass windows. Venetian blinds had been let down and through them she could see the panorama of the city glittering with a myriad lights below her. And yet for all that they were in the heart of the city, it was silent up here, silent and isolated, and remote like the cabin of an airliner. One could not fail to get an inflated feeling of one's own importance living here, thought Julie ruefully.

She was startled into awareness by the closing of the door and swinging round to face Robert Pemberton she paused to wonder how long he had been standing there, watching her. He was not wearing a dinner jacket but had shed the informal suede for a charcoal grey lounge suite that fitted his lean body closely, accentuating the length of his legs and the hard muscles beneath the rippling material. From the dampness of his hair, she guessed he had recently stepped out of the shower.

His gaze flickered over her for a moment, taking in the fragility of her appearance, and then with a casual movement of his shoulders he walked across to where an opened cabinet displayed an assortment of bottles.

'What will you drink?' he inquired, turning his back on her and uncorking the whisky bottle, scooping ice out of its container, chinking it into a glass.

Julie took a deep breath. 'Gin and tonic, please,' she replied, taking care that her voice should reveal none of her thoughts.

Robert made the drink and turning walked across to hand it to her. As he did so Julie caught his gaze, and taking the initiative, she said: 'Are you going to tell me now why we've been brought here?'

Robert hesitated, rubbing his palms together where the condensation on the chilled glass had dampened them. 'Does it matter?' he asked briefly. 'I can assure you my motives were purely unselfish ones.'

'What am I supposed to gather from that remark?'

'What I say. My mother is incapable of accommodating you. Naturally as Michael's widow you are welcome here.'

'You don't sound very welcoming.' Julie sipped her drink to hide her nervousness.

'Don't I?' Robert made an indifferent gesture. 'I'm sorry.'

'You're not sorry at all!' Julie burst out, and then regretted it. Taking another trembling breath, she hastened on: 'What I can't understand is why your mother should have written and offered Emma and me a home now that – now that she's alone, and not really mean it.'

'Would you have come if you'd known it was I who was offering you a home?' inquired Robert coldly.

Julie pressed her lips together. 'Of course not.'

'There you are, then.' Robert turned away to get his own drink and Julie gave a helpless gasp.

'You mean I was brought here under false pretences?'

'Stop being dramatic, Julie. It was necessary that you should be brought back here. This was the only way.'

Julie was indignant. 'But why was it necessary? I – your mother never wanted me when – when Michael was alive. Why should she want me now that Michael is dead?'

Robert swallowed half his whisky at a gulp and then looked at her again. 'My mother is changing for dinner. We don't have much time. I want you to tell me what happened – before she comes back.'

'About Michael's death, you mean?'

'Naturally.'

Julie bent her head. 'Why naturally? You haven't shown much interest up until now.'

Robert uttered an expletive. 'I don't want to waste time arguing with you, Julie. Just tell me the facts. I could hardly discuss this in front of Emma, could I? And my mother's too emotional about it for us to have a coherent conversation in front of her.'

Julie looked up indignantly. 'And I'm not emotional, of course. He – he was my husband, that's all!'

Robert reached for a cigar from a box on a low table, lighting it with suppressed violence. She could see it in the hardening of his facial muscles, in the grim way his teeth held the cigar, in the impatient flick of the table lighter.

'What do you want me to say, Julie?' he asked, straightening. 'Do you want to hear platitudes from me? I think not.

We'd both know they were not sincere. But I did love my brother, whatever you may think, and I want to know about his death. Now – will you tell me?'

Julie turned her back on him. She couldn't bear to look at him while she spoke about something that was still painful to her.

'You – you had the doctor's reports,' she said tightly. 'You didn't come to see him.'

'No. A fact I bitterly regret.' His voice was harsh.

'Do you?' Julie sounded sceptical, but she didn't pursue it. 'Well, I don't know what more you want to hear. I didn't know about the first attack, if that's of any interest to you. Michael forced the doctor to keep the truth to himself. I thought he was overworked, tired. I never suspected the heat was affecting his heart. He had put on weight, of course. He drank quite a lot, but then so did everybody. In any event, I don't believe Michael took it really seriously himself. But when the second attack came, so soon after the first, he hadn't the strength to fight it . . .' She broke off, fighting back the emotionalism that threatened to overwhelm her. Michael had been such a young man, a good man; he had not deserved to die.

'I see.' She heard Robert move and pour himself another drink. 'Was he in much pain, before he died, I mean?'

Julie shook her head. 'Oh, no. The drugs they prescribed kept him more or less comatose. Sometimes he didn't even recognize me. But I think he guessed it was hopeless.'

'You should have sent for me.' Robert's voice was abrupt. 'You knew I would have come if I had known – if I had guessed—'

Julie looked unseeingly through the slats of the venetian blind. 'He wouldn't allow me to send for anybody. I don't know why. But I couldn't go against his wishes.'

Robert walked across the width of the lounge to her side. She hadn't looked round, but she was conscious of him with every fibre of her being. 'I would have come to the funeral,' he said shortly. 'But I was out of the country when your cable arrived. And naturally the burial took place so much more quickly than it would have done here.'

'Yes.' Julie finished her drink and moved away from the window. Away from *him*. 'Is that all?'

Robert swung round, his expression hardening at the resignation in her voice. 'Are you so indifferent?' he muttered.

'*Indifferent!*' Julie put a hand to her throat defensively. 'My God! You think *I'm* indifferent?'

'Well, aren't you? I can't see any tears in those limpid green eyes!'

Julie found it difficult to breathe suddenly. 'That's a foul thing to say!'

'Why? Am I mistaken? Are you really the bereft widow?'

Julie stared at him for a long moment, anger strengthening her weakening resolve. 'How dare you speak to me like that!' she demanded fiercely. 'I didn't ask to come here! I didn't ask to be patronized by the powerful Pemberton family! I want nothing from any of you – *you*, least of all!'

Robert's face paled slightly under his tan and she realized that for once she had succeeded in really getting under his skin. 'That's right, Julie,' he snarled. 'Show your true colours! Show what a selfish coarse little bitch you really are!'

Julie took a step forward. She wanted to slap that sneering violence from his face once and for all. But even as she moved the door opened to admit Lucy Pemberton.

Lucy was wearing a long black gown of heavy silk, several strings of pearls about her still youthful throat. For all she was almost sixty, life had aged her little, and looking at her now Julie found it hard to believe that she had not been well enough to come to the airport to meet them.

But it was no use harbouring grudges. In a few days, a week at the most, she would find somewhere for herself and Emma to live, and then she would be free of the Pemberton family for good.

'Hello,' said Lucy, when she saw them both. 'You're still here, Robert?' Was that a note of reproof in her voice? 'I thought your appointment was for seven-thirty. It's gone that already, you know.'

Robert stubbed out the cigar he had been smoking and dropped it carelessly into the ashtray. 'There's no hurry, Mother,' he remarked, in complete control of himself again.

'I'm not sure Pamela would agree with you, darling.' There was definitely a note of reproof now, and a brief dismissing glance in Julie's direction. 'You must meet Pamela, Julie. Pamela Hillingdon. You may have heard of the family. She and Robert are getting married in the spring.'

Julie managed to appear unmoved by this news. 'Really,' she said evenly. 'But I doubt whether I'll ever have that opportunity. She and I no doubt move in different circles.'

Robert had been reaching for the handle of the door, but at her words he turned abruptly to face her, his eyes narrowing. 'I don't understand what you mean, Julie,' he stated flatly, and his mother drew her brows together in delicate bewilderment.

'You're not going to be difficult, Julie, I hope,' she exclaimed, and received a quelling glance from her son which Julie found hard to comprehend.

'Well?' Robert demanded. 'Exactly what are you saying, Julie?'

Julie felt her cheeks colouring in spite of her determination to stay cool. 'Surely it's obvious,' she stated steadily. 'I – well – Emma and I can't live here. Within the next few days, I intend to look around for a job and somewhere for Emma and myself to live—'

'What?' Lucy put a trembling hand to her temples and sank down weakly into the nearest chair. 'Oh, Julie, you can't be serious!'

'It doesn't matter whether she is or otherwise,' snapped Robert obliquely. 'She hasn't yet been informed of the facts of the case.'

'What facts?' Julie pressed her palms together apprehensively.

Lucy looked up at her son. 'You didn't tell her?'

'I didn't get the chance.' Robert raked a hand through the thick darkness of his hair. When he was disturbed as he was now it was painfully easy to remember the last confrontation she had had with him, and Julie bent her head to avoid the cold brilliance of those grey eyes.

'Will you please tell me what I'm supposed to be told?' Julie wondered how long her legs would continue to support her. 'Is there some reason why I should not be permitted to do as I like?' She looked up suddenly, her eyes guarded. 'Because if there is, I shall fight it.'

'Oh, Julie, please.' Lucy fanned herself with one hand. 'Don't be difficult! We only want to do what's best for – for you, and for Emma.'

Robert flicked back his cuff and glanced at the broad gold watch on his wrist and Julie stiffened. 'Don't let me keep you from your appointment,' she exclaimed. 'Just say what you have to say and go!'

Robert's eyes glittered. She knew that had they been alone there would have been things said which they might both have regretted later, although she doubted that Robert ever did anything he might regret.

'Michael left a will,' he said at last.

'I know that. He left his shares in the company to the family. So what? I don't need anything—'

'Don't talk rubbish!' Robert lost control for a moment and turning away he poured himself another drink, swallowing half of it while his mother clicked her tongue irritably.

'Can't we all keep our tempers?' she asked, through tight lips.

Robert turned back, the glass in his hand. 'Very well, I'll try and be brief. Michael left his shares in the company to the family to be kept in trust for Emma until she's twenty-one. Until then, she is left in my guardianship.'

'*No!*' The word was torn incredulously from Julie's lips.

'Yes,' said Robert inflexibly. 'And I shouldn't advise you to fight that!'

Julie out put a hand, catching the back of a chair to support herself. She couldn't believe her ears. Michael couldn't have made such a will. Not knowing . . . not knowing . . .

She closed her eyes. She thought she was going to faint and she heard Lucy say: 'Good heavens, Robert, she's going to pass out!' before strong hands she hadn't the will to shake off were lowering her firmly into a chair. Resting her head against the soft upholstery the feeling of faintness receded, and she opened her eyes again to find Robert about to put a glass of some amber liquid into her hand.

'Drink this,' he advised. 'It will make you feel better.'

Julie's breathing was short and constricted. 'Nothing will make me feel better,' she retorted childishly. 'Take it away!'

Robert ignored her, pressing the glass into her hand so that she was forced to take it or spill it over her dress. 'Don't be foolish!' he said coldly, straightening.

Julie looked at the glass unseeingly. She was trembling violently, and her mind was running round in circles trying to dismiss what had just been said as impossible.

'You must go, Robert.' Lucy was looking quite agitated now. 'I can handle this.'

'Can you?' Robert looked sceptical.

'Of course. Julie must be made to understand her position. As Michael's widow—'

'Oh, stop talking about me as though I wasn't here!' cried Julie, struggling up in her seat.

Robert looked at her dispassionately. 'Well?' he said. 'Are you prepared to discuss this reasonably?'

'Reasonably? Reasonably? How can I be reasonable? Emma's my child—'

'But my responsibility,' inserted Robert.

Julie shook her head helplessly. 'Why would Michael do such a thing to me?' she asked brokenly.

'Don't be maudlin,' Lucy Pemberton was impatient. 'My son had the sense to realize that should anything happen to him, the person most suited to bringing up his child should be his own brother.'

'But I'm her mother!' Julie protested.

'Yes. And without us, what could you give her?' Lucy sniffed. 'You never had anything—'

'Money's not everything!' cried Julie, gripping the arm of her chair with her free hand.

'I didn't mention money.'

'No, but that's what you meant, didn't you?'

'There are other – qualities—'

'What do you mean?' Julie caught her breath.

'Oh, for God's sake!' Robert ran a hand round the back of his neck, smoothing the hair that brushed his collar. 'Let's stop this arguing! It doesn't matter for what reason Michael made his decision. The decision's made now, and we must make the best of it.'

Julie thrust the untouched glass of brandy on to a side table. The smell had been enough for her. Then she got unsteadily to her feet. 'I don't want to make the best of it,' she said. 'I suppose that was why you wrote asking me to come here, wasn't it?' She was looking at Lucy now. 'You knew if you told me the truth I might not agree.'

Robert heaved a sigh. 'It might be true to say that my mother wrote to you to make things easier for you, but regardless of whether you like it or not, the will stands and will be adhered to whatever the circumstances.'

Julie swallowed hard. 'I could contest it.'

'You could,' Robert agreed dryly. 'But as my brother also states that you shall be cared for, too, I hardly think any lawyer would take the case.' He made an impatient gesture. 'What have you to contest?'

Julie moved her head slowly from side to side. 'There – there must be ways,' she said unsteadily. 'I – I can't be forced to live here.'

'Agreed. *You* can live where you like. But if you want to remain with Emma, then you'll have to do what I want you to do.'

'Which is?' Julie's lip curled.

'Remain here until the house I've bought in the country is prepared, and then live there, with Emma, and with a young governess I've already employed for her.'

Julie was aghast. 'You mean – you mean you've already bought this house – employed this woman – all on the strength of my agreement?'

Robert shook his head. 'On the strength of Michael's will, Julie.'

'And – and you? You're getting married soon. How – how can you care for Emma?'

'Until my marriage, I intend to spend most week-ends with her. Afterwards, no doubt some arrangement for weekends or holidays can be arranged. I'm not unreasonable, Julie. You'll still have your daughter.'

Julie uttered an angry cry. 'When *you* say so! Is that it? And what if this fiancée of yours, this – this Pamela – doesn't care for the idea?'

'Pamela already knows of Robert's commitment,' stated

Lucy complacently. 'Really, Julie, I do think you're behaving very ungratefully. One would imagine Robert was about to kidnap Emma and prevent you from having any kind of access. I think he's being most generous.'

Julie shook her head. She was helpless in the face of their calm detachment, and an awful feeling of despair was gripping her heart. She was tied, tied hand and foot, and Michael was responsible. But why? Why had he done this? Surely he of all people must have known she could not bear to feel beholden to Robert . . .

Suddenly the telephone began to ring. The shrill sound was startling in the silence which had fallen. Robert hesitated a moment, and then walked swiftly across the room and lifted the receiver.

'Yes?' he said abruptly, and then his expression relaxed. 'Oh, hello, Pamela. Yes, yes, I know. I'm sorry. Something came up. They've arrived, yes. I know – I know – I'll be leaving shortly.'

Julie turned away, and as she did so Halbird came into the room from the direction of the kitchen, an enormous white apron covering his dark trousers and waistcoat.

Seeing that Robert was using the telephone, he addressed himself to Lucy. 'Dinner is ready, madam. Shall I begin to serve?'

Lucy got regally out of her chair. 'Thank you, Halbird. We'll be through in five minutes.'

'Yes, madam.' Halbird withdrew again and Lucy looked resignedly at her daughter-in-law.

'You'll have gathered that Robert is dining out this evening,' she said, in an undertone. 'I hope we can have dinner without any further melodramatics.'

Julie stared at her. 'This was what you wanted, wasn't it?' she demanded heatedly. 'You never wanted me to marry – Michael, and now you're determined to control Emma's life, too.'

'Just as you were determined to marry into this family,' snapped Lucy, all vestige of tolerance disappearing. 'You couldn't have Robert, so you made do with Michael!'

Julie's lips parted on a gasp of horror, and then without another word she brushed past her mother-in-law and opening the panelled doors left the room.

In the comparative peace of her own room she stood in the centre of the floor fighting for control. This would not do. She would achieve nothing by being emotional. She needed time. Time to think this out; to adjust to her new circumstances; to endeavour to salvage something from the wreckage of her hopes for the future. By behaving foolishly now she could destroy any chance of herself and Emma leading a normal life.

She looked down at her hands. The palms were damp, and there was a film of sweat on her forehead. The thought of food, of sitting down at a table with Lucy Pemberton was intolerable right now, and on impulse she unzipped her dress and was about to step out of it preparatory to taking a cooling shower when the door of her room opened without warning and Robert stood on the threshold glaring at her.

'What the hell do you think you're doing?' he bit out savagely. 'Halbird is waiting to serve dinner, and I've got to go out.'

Julie held the two sides of her gown together behind her back, aware that his painful scrutiny missed little. 'I'm not stopping anything,' she said. 'Let your mother have her dinner. I couldn't eat a thing.'

'For God's sake, Julie, be reasonable!' Robert cupped the back of his neck with his hands as though it ached. 'I'm trying to be patient. Now, I'm asking you – not telling you, or commanding you, but *asking* you to go and eat dinner with my mother and try and behave as though none of this had ever happened.'

Julie's long dark lashes glittered with unshed tears.

'You've got to be joking!' she choked.

'But don't you see? It need not have happened this way. If you'd only been prepared to accept—'

'Your charity, Robert?' She held up her head. 'No, thanks, I could never accept that.'

'Then in God's name, what do you plan to do?' Robert advanced into the room, half-closed the door, and then opened it again as though having second thoughts.

Julie stood her ground. She would not allow him to intimidate her. She *must* not. 'I – I don't know yet. Maybe I'll have to accept your plans for Emma, but I – I don't intend to remain dependent upon you.'

Robert frowned. 'What will you do?'

'I'll get a job. If you've employed a governess for Emma, my presence is going to be incidental for most, or at least part, of the day. What do you expect me to do, Robert? Twiddle my thumbs?'

'I expect you to behave as the widow of Michael Pemberton should behave – with respect, and decorum.' Robert's gaze raked her. 'What have you done all these years in Malaya? How did you fill your days?'

Julie moved uncomfortably. 'That was different. I – I had a home. A husband and family to care for.' She turned aside, unable to bear the penetration of those grey eyes, unknowingly revealing to him the vulnerable nape of her neck, and the pale tan of the skin of her back where her dress was unfastened.

'You still have a family,' muttered Robert harshly. Then more huskily: 'God, Julie, why are you so thin? How long is it since you had a good meal?'

Julie realized her state of undress with some embarrassment and turned to him abruptly. 'Will you please go away and leave me alone? I – I'm tired. I'd like to go to bed.'

'Julie—' he was beginning, when there was a sound behind them and looking beyond Robert, Julie saw her mother-in-law standing in the doorway.

'Robert!' his mother exclaimed in annoyance. 'Are you still here? I thought you must have gone. I was just coming to see what Julie – was – doing—' Her voice slowed as she, too, took in Julie's appearance. 'Good heavens, what is going on?'

'Nothing's going on!' snapped Julie, unable to stand any more of this. 'Will you go? Both of you? I'm not hungry, and I am tired. I just want to be left alone.'

Robert swung on his heel and walked out of the room. 'I'm leaving now,' he said to his mother. 'Good night.'

'Good night, darling.' Lucy watched him walk away along the corridor and then as the outer door slammed, she turned back to Julie. 'I gather you're not joining me for dinner.'

'That's right.' Julie felt unutterably weary. 'Is it too much to ask that I should be left alone?'

Lucy made an indifferent movement of her shoulders. 'Of course not. But don't think I'm a fool, will you, Julie?'

Julie stared at her. 'What do you mean?'

Lucy's gaze dropped down her body insolently. 'Must I elucidate?' she queried coldly. 'Entertaining Robert in that state!'

Julie gasped. 'I was not entertaining Robert!' she denied hotly. 'I – I – he just walked in on me!'

Lucy shook her head slowly. 'I think not. My son knows better than to walk unannounced into a young woman's bedroom.'

Julie spread a hand helplessly. 'Go away,' she said appealingly, 'please!'

Lucy hesitated only a moment longer and then she nodded briefly and walked away without speaking again.

Julie almost ran across to the door and slammed it heavily, leaning back against it with trembling limbs. Oh, God, she thought despairingly. How was she ever going to bear it?

CHAPTER THREE

THE next morning Julie was awakened by Emma bouncing on the end of her bed, and she opened her eyes reluctantly, aware of an indefinable feeling of ominous apprehension. The events of the previous day came flooding back to her, and for a moment she longed to bury her head under the covers and stay where she was.

Then Emma's bright little face swam into focus and she knew she could not spoil her pleasure in the day.

Emma was dressed already. Someone had supervised what she should put on, for the trews and sweater she was wearing had not been unpacked the night before, and her long straight hair had been combed into order.

Julie struggled into a sitting position. 'What time is it?' she asked, reaching for her watch which she had laid on the bedside table when she went to bed. 'Heavens! It's after ten. Why didn't you wake me earlier?'

'Grandma said you were tired, and Uncle Robert said you would feel better after a long sleep.'

Julie smoothed her hair behind her ears. 'You mean – they're up?'

'Well, Grandma's not dressed yet. I had breakfast with her, in her room, and Uncle Robert came in later and asked what I usually wore.'

'I see.' Julie reached for her dressing-gown. 'And did you wash and clean your teeth?'

'Yes. Uncle Robert showed me where everything was. And that man – Halbird—'

'*Mr.* Halbird, darling,' inserted Julie automatically, sliding out of bed.

Emma shrugged indifferently. 'Well, whoever he is – he

unpacked my things and we put them all away in my own drawers.' She smiled. 'He said I was very grown up for my age.'

Julie sighed. 'Who did?'

'Halbird – Mr. Halbird, I mean.'

Julie shook her head. 'Well, I wish you'd woken me. Where is everyone now?'

'Grandma's getting dressed and Uncle Robert's gone to get the car out. We're going out.'

Julie, on her way to the bathroom, swung round. 'Who is?'

'Uncle Robert and me,' said Emma ungrammatically. She smiled complacently. 'We're going to see the new house.'

Julie stared at her for a long moment. 'You're sure Uncle Robert said he's taking you.'

'Of course.' Emma jumped off the bed indignantly. 'He said he'd show me Buckingham Palace, too.'

Julie pushed open the bathroom door, and going inside turned on the shower. Then she secured her hair beneath a plastic cap and took off her dressing-gown and nightdress. As she stepped under the shower, she felt a disturbing sense of envy at Emma's completely natural adaptation to these new circumstances. What it was to be a child, to accept everything on its face value without searching beneath the surface for ulterior motives.

Later, she came out of the bathroom wrapped in a towelling bathrobe to shift Emma out while she dressed.

'When are you leaving?' she asked, trying to keep the possessiveness out of her voice.

Emma shrugged. 'Soon, I suppose. When you're ready, I guess.'

'Me?' Julie swung round on her. 'What have I to do with it?'

'Well, you're coming, too, aren't you?' Emma looked puzzled.

Julie sighed. 'Did Uncle Robert say that, too.'

Emma considered for a moment. 'Well, he told me to come and wake you and ask you if you'd like some coffee.'

'Did he indeed?' Julie gave her daughter a resigned stare. 'And did you?'

'Did I what?'

'Ask me if I wanted coffee?'

Emma hung her head. 'I forgot.'

'Well, I do, so scoot. And don't come back. I'll come when I'm dressed.'

Emma's mouth tilted at the corners. 'You're not cross, are you?'

'Of course not. Run along. I've got to get dressed.'

'All right.' Emma skipped to the door. Then she stopped hesitantly. 'You do like it here, don't you, Mummy? I mean – you like Uncle Robert and Grandma and – and everyone?'

'How could I not?' exclaimed Julie impatiently. 'Go on, stop worrying, everything's fine.'

It wasn't until Julie was pulling on close-fitting corded pants in a rather attractive shade of purple that she paused to wonder why Emma should have asked her such a strange question. Then she shrugged and went on dressing. No doubt the child was sensitive to atmosphere, and there had been plenty of that in Robert's car yesterday.

She put on a fine wool cream sweater with the pants, leaving her throat to rise smoothly from the open neckline. Her hair hung silkily about her shoulders, and the only make-up she used was a faint eye-shadow and a colourless lustre for her lips.

When she was satisfied with her appearance, she left her room and walked determinedly along the hall to the lounge. The hall, now she had time to notice it, was wide and attractive, papered in gold damask with several examples of French Impressionist painting lining the walls. The carpet was blue and gold, and there was a gilt-edged occasional table and two chairs to match beside it.

The double doors which led into the lounge were at the end of the hall near the single panelled door which opened into the lobby they had entered the previous afternoon.

Summoning all her courage, she pressed open the lounge doors and entered the room, closing them behind her. Unlike the night before, it was not deserted now. Emma and her grandmother were seated on a low couch near the windows, looking at a picture book from which Lucy was reading a story, while Halbird was busily dusting the bookshelves which flanked the hi-fi equipment at the far end of the room. He looked up as she came in, and his smile made up for Lucy's apparent ignorance of her presence.

'Good morning, Mrs. Pemberton,' he said, stopping what he was doing. 'If you'll come through to the dining-room, I've prepared a little something for you.'

'Oh – oh, you shouldn't have bothered.' Julie glanced doubtfully at her mother-in-law and Emma, and this time they both looked up.

'Grandma's reading me a story,' said Emma innocently.

'Good morning, Julie.' Lucy's greeting was less than cordial. 'Did you sleep well?'

'Thank you, yes.' Julie glanced at Halbird, who was standing waiting for her. 'Excuse me, I'll just go and have some coffee.'

Lucy returned her attention to the book for a moment and then looked up again. 'I thought we might go shopping this afternoon,' she said with reluctance. 'This child is hopelessly ill equipped for a winter in England.'

Julie stiffened. 'Most of Emma's clothes are in the trunks coming by sea—'

'I know that. The trunks have already arrived.'

'Where are they, then?' Julie looked bewildered.

'They're at the house, of course,' replied Lucy. 'There was no point in bringing them here, was there? You won't be staying here that long.'

Julie felt exasperated. 'But I can't possibly manage more than a couple of days with what I've brought with me.'

Lucy shrugged indifferently. 'You can always buy a few things for yourself.' She raised her eyebrows. 'I doubt very much whether the clothes you wore in Malaya will be particularly useful here. Apart from the change of climate, you'll be expected to dress fashionably. And as Michael's widow ...' She dabbed her eyes suddenly, and Julie turned away.

She couldn't bear to say anything more. She didn't trust herself to do so. Not without causing another row. Emma was looking from one to the other of them with evident concern, and besides, this was neither the time nor the place to discuss Michael.

Instead, she followed Halbird through the door he indicated and found herself in a large, well lit dining-room. The dining-table was long and highly polished, and a single place had been laid at one end for her. There was coffee, and warm rolls, toast and marmalade, and scrambled eggs keeping warm over a burner. Julie felt a ridiculous prick of tears at Halbird's thoughtfulness.

Turning to him, she exclaimed helplessly: 'This wasn't necessary, you know.'

The man smiled. 'You had no dinner last evening,' he pointed out. 'I'm sure you must be hungry. Everything looks so much better if the stomach's not crying out for sustenance.'

Julie glanced at him sharply, but his expression was benign. All the same, she sensed Halbird's sympathy, and was unreasonably glad of it. It was reassuring to know that one person at least did not resent her being here.

And, in fact, she made a good breakfast. Despite the

emotional state of her nerves she was hungry, she found, and after a plate of scrambled eggs, some toast and marmalade, and several cups of strong black coffee she did indeed feel more ready to face the world in general and the Pemberton's in particular.

She was chatting to Halbird about the changes she had seen the day before in London when Robert came in. This morning he was wearing dark green suede pants and a matching shirt in a slightly lighter shade together with a dark brown leather waistcoat that hung loosely from his shoulders. He looked big and powerful and disturbing, and Julie had to steel herself not to stare at him.

'Well?' he said abruptly, interrupting their conversation. 'Are you ready?'

Julie looked up then. 'Ready?' She raised her dark eyebrows. 'Ready for what?'

Robert glanced meaningfully at Halbird, and the manservant nodded politely and left the room, returning to the lounge to finish his dusting, Julie supposed.

'Didn't Emma advise you of the arrangements?' Robert was distant.

Julie sighed and rose to her feet, smoothing down the cream sweater over her slim hips. 'Not really. She said something about you and her going to see the new house.'

'Precisely.' Robert surveyed her intently. 'Naturally you'll want to see your new home, too.'

'Oh, thank you. That was thoughtful.' The sarcasm was audible in Julie's voice.

Robert uttered an expletive. 'For God's sake, Julie, we can't go on like this. Look – can't we at least behave civilly in front of Emma? I'm getting a bit sick of this constant bickering.'

'So am I!' Julie flared.

'Well, then.'

Julie shook her head. 'It's easy for you, isn't it? You're

having everything your own way, aren't you?'

Robert let his breath out on a heavy sigh. 'Oh, stop it, Julie!' He ran a hand over his hair impatiently. 'What do you want me to say? I'm doing my best to be tolerant—'

'*Tolerant!*' Julie was indignant. 'What have you to be tolerant of?'

'You!' he snapped shortly. 'Do you think given the choice, I would have accepted this situation?'

Julie held up her head. 'It's what your mother wanted.'

'But not what I wanted!' Robert's voice was harsh. 'Believe me, Julie, I prayed I'd never have to see you again!'

Julie felt the hot colour burn up her throat and into her face. 'I – I bet you did,' she faltered unconvincingly.

'Oh, Julie!' There was an agonized kind of exasperation in his voice now. 'This is getting us nowhere. Look, what's past is past. We've both got to accept that, haven't we? And Michael chose that you and Emma should be put into my care – let's at least try and remember that.'

Julie bent her head. 'How could I forget it?' she whispered tremulously.

Robert made a helpless gesture, and then moving closer put his hand on her shoulder as if to show that he understood the grief she was feeling. But Julie flinched away from his touch as though his cool flesh had burned her, and his jaw tightened angrily before he flung himself away from her and through the door into the lounge.

Julie stood where he had left her, trembling violently. His solicitude had been so unexpected, and she would not have believed it could have such a profound effect on her. She had expected to feel a kind of painful nostalgia at seeing Robert again, but nothing she had imagined had prepared her for this instant emotionalism whenever he came near her, and when he had touched her, her flesh had melted beneath his fingers exactly as it had used to do.

She pressed the palms of her hands to her burning cheeks.

This was crazy. She wasn't an impressionable teenager any longer. She was a woman, a woman of twenty-six, who had been married for almost six years. How could she react so intensely to such an indifferent gesture? Where was the control she had always prided herself on possessing? Whatever must he have thought of her?

Suddenly the door to the lounge opened and Emma appeared, her expression changing to one of concern as she took in Julie's obvious distress. 'What's the matter, Mummy? Are you crying about Daddy again?'

Emma's words sobered her. 'I'm not crying, darling. I – I got something in my eye, that's all.'

Emma frowned for a moment, and then seemed to accept the explanation. 'We're waiting for you,' she said. 'Are you coming?'

Julie realized that Emma was now wearing the red anorak she had brought with her from Rhatoon, and was obviously ready to go out. Nodding, she followed Emma back into the lounge to find Robert in conversation with his mother. He had put on a sheepskin jacket which added to his height and bulk, and he glanced round impatiently when he saw Julie was still not ready.

'I really don't see why Julie needs to go,' Lucy Pemberton was saying. 'I understood you were only going to see the contractors, Robert.'

'I am. But as Julie is to live there I don't see why she shouldn't see the place.' He turned to his sister-in-law. 'Do you want to go?'

Julie hesitated. Of course she wanted to go. But a morning spent in Robert's company could be disastrous to her peace of mind. Nevertheless, a morning spent with Lucy Pemberton was likely to be much worse.

'Of course I want to go,' she said, infusing a note of casual interest into her voice, endeavouring to show him she was in complete control of herself again. 'If you'd woken me earlier, I'd not have kept you waiting so long.'

Robert looked relieved. 'Fine. Well, get a coat. It's fine, but it's damn cold, believe me.'

'I do.' Julie nodded, and with lightening steps left the room.

The only coat she had to wear at the moment was the sable fur which had been her only extravagance, and which she had bought on the advice of a friend, before leaving Kuala Lumpur. It had seemed ridiculous buying such a garment out there, but she had been glad of its warmth yesterday afternoon getting off the aircraft. So she put it on, grimacing at the purple trousers as she did so. Actually, though, they didn't look at all bad together, the coat being only a little longer than thigh length anyway. Strands of her hair looked pale and attractive against the upturned collar, and she decided there was no trace now of her earlier distress.

When she returned to the lounge, Robert stubbed out the cigar he had been smoking and walked abruptly towards the outer door followed by an excited Emma. Lucy clicked her tongue in obvious annoyance.

'And when will you be back?' she demanded. 'It's nearly eleven o'clock now!' She gave Julie a crushing stare. 'I thought you said you wanted to go shopping.'

Julie was taken aback. It had not been her suggestion that they might visit the stores. 'We can go another day,' she replied, glancing awkwardly at Robert to observe his reaction.

'I see.' Lucy tilted her head to register her disapproval and unwillingly Julie recalled her insinuations of the night before.

Robert had opened the lounge door and was looking impatient. 'Are you coming or are you not?' he inquired, with cold politeness.

Julie pressed her lips together, and then with a slight

movement of her shoulders she walked towards him. 'I'm coming,' she averred firmly.

After allowing Emma to scramble into the back, Julie took her seat in the front of the Aston Martin with a curious feeling of relief. She refused to consider what Lucy might say when next they were alone together. She must try and prevent her from intimidating her as she seemed so easily capable of doing. She was only a woman, after all, not an ogre, and surely she ought to be able to cope with that.

Robert slid into his seat beside her, slamming his door and starting the powerful engine. With him came a cold draught of air and the more intimate odours like shaving cream and soap, and the clean, warm, male smell of his body.

Trying to distract herself, Julie wondered what he did with his time these days. Six years ago he had been an active member of the company, but perhaps now he had given that up. And soon he would have a wife to consider. The muscles of her stomach contracted. She would not think of things like that. But it was extraordinarily difficult not to do so with Robert sitting here in the car beside her, touchable, and yet untouchable, so near, and yet so distant. What was this woman like whom his mother seemed to consider so suitable, so acceptable for him? Was she beautiful? How long had he known her? How late had he been with her last night?

She had not been paying much attention to their whereabouts, but now she was aware that Emma was asking him questions about the places they were passing, and she realized Robert was taking them on a swift tour of the city. Looking about her, she recognized the shops of Oxford Street, and just at that moment, Emma said: 'Isn't this exciting, Mummy? Uncle Robert's going to drive up the Mall soon to Buckingham Palace!'

Julie managed a smile. 'So long as you don't expect to see the Queen,' she observed dryly. 'She didn't know you were coming, you see.'

Emma gurgled with laughter at this and Julie bent her head.

After driving past the palace, and allowing Emma to exclaim with delight at the guards outside, they turned into Birdcage Walk and crossed the river at Westminster Bridge to allow her to see the Houses of Parliament. Then the car picked up speed and Julie glanced inquiringly at her brother-in-law.

'Am I allowed to ask where we're going?'

Robert slowed as they encountered a snarl-up of traffic and looked at her. 'Of course. We're on the Dartford road. On our way to Thorpe Hulme.'

'Thorpe Hulme?' Julie frowned. 'I've never heard of it.'

'Why should you? It's not a particularly well known place. Just a village, in fact.'

'And — and that's where this — this house is?'

'That's right.'

'I see.' Julie looked out at the passing landscape. 'And what made you choose Thorpe Hulme?'

Robert hesitated, his fingers tightening on the wheel. 'When Pamela and I get married, we hope to live at Farnborough. Her parents live at Orpington, and she doesn't want to live too far away from them. Thorpe Hulme is approximately ten miles from Farnborough.'

Julie digested this slowly. So when Robert was married he would be living only ten miles away. The idea was intolerable. She had a sudden and intense longing for the peace and tranquillity of the bungalow outside Rhatoon.

But knowing something was expected of her, she folded her gloves in her lap, and said: 'I should have thought the apartment would have been a more suitable home for you. Close to the office, and so on. Or don't you take any active part in the proceedings any longer?'

47

The traffic was opening out again, and Robert negotiated a fleet of slow-moving lorries before replying: 'Naturally I still work for the company. Being a sybarite for the rest of my life doesn't appeal to me. Although naturally, once I'm married, I shall curtail my commitments abroad.'

Julie's lips tightened. 'My! You've changed!' she remarked.

Robert flashed her an impatient look. 'I thought we had agreed not to argue in front of the child,' he exclaimed.

'I'm not arguing,' Julie contradicted, and then realized she was doing just that. 'Well, anyway, an observation can hardly be called an argument just because it's not to your liking!'

Robert's face registered his displeasure, but he made no further comment, which made Julie chide herself for creating another open rift between them. Why couldn't she just accept the situation as it was, and not torture herself by thoughts of what might have been?

She glanced at Emma and her daughter slid her arms round her neck from behind and hugged her spontaneously. Julie blinked back tears of self-pity. She had chosen her road in life. She had insisted on avoiding the humiliation of appealing to Robert for his help at a time when she most needed it. So how could she now inwardly rebuke him for something of which he had known nothing? And yet he was to blame...

They left the main road and followed a winding country road for some distance before reaching the village of Thorpe Hulme. Even Julie, in her depressed state of mind, could see that it was a pretty place, and Emma pointed excitedly to the pond in the middle of the green where several ducks swam contentedly.

There was a row of cottages flanking the green, two pubs, a village school, a couple of small religious establishments, and a shop which looked as though it might sell anything and everything. There were trees everywhere, although now these were bare of leaves and were mere skeletons of their summer selves.

Robert made various observations for Emma's benefit, and then drove on through the village to the outskirts. At the end of the main street, he turned into a lane which in turn led through double wrought iron gates, now standing open, and up the drive to a house that was temporarily concealed by the privet hedging the drive. Several vans of the various contractors making alterations to the place stood on the forecourt, but it was the house itself which caught Julie's attention.

It was one of those small Georgian houses that were presently costing the earth to buy. Lots of small windows, slightly bow-fronted to the main rooms, gave it a charm all its own, and as it was painted white and framed by pine trees it could not have looked more attractive.

Robert brought the car to a halt beside the other vehicles and then looked across at Julie, drawing in his lower lip with his even white teeth. 'Well?' he said, and there was neither reproach nor enthusiasm in his voice.

Julie was staring at the house. She seemed to be finding it difficult to gather her thoughts. Shaking her head, she thrust open her door and stepped out into the frosty air. Hugging the sable coat about her, she was scarcely conscious of Robert getting out of the car and helping Emma to climb out of the back until Emma scampered up to her and said:

'Is this where we're going to live, Mummy? Oh, isn't it super?'

She ran on ahead, not waiting for an answer, and Julie became aware of Robert at her side. Looking up at his enigmatic face, she made a helpless gesture. 'It's beautiful,' she said. 'However did you find it?'

Robert thrust his hands into the pockets of his sheepskin coat. 'It came on the market about three months ago, about the time Michael died, in fact. I bought it because I liked it.'

'But not with me in mind,' Julie prompted.

Robert strode on ahead, glancing back over his shoulder. 'Does it matter?' he asked, and joining Emma he thrust open the door and entered the house.

Julie followed more slowly. She wanted to look and digest the knowledge that this was to be her home, possibly for the rest of her life! But no. Once Emma was old enough to leave home, then she would leave, too. She could always take a flat, providing she could afford one. It was strange how the idea of ever marrying again never even entered her head... Not now...

Robert and Emma were standing in the hall. Robert was talking to two men in overalls, and there was a smell of new paint and wallpaper pervading the atmosphere. Surprisingly, though, the house was warm, and she realized the central heating was working.

She waited patiently until he had finished asking about various improvements which were being made, and then when the men went away he turned to her.

'They've nearly finished,' he explained. 'There's no furnishings in the place, of course, but you can look around if you'd like to.'

Julie nodded eagerly. 'I've love to.' Then she hesitated a moment. 'Oh – oh, and Robert?'

'Yes?' His expression was not encouraging.

'I – thank you.'

Robert's eyes narrowed. 'You're thanking me?' he queried mockingly, and Julie turned abruptly away.

'You said we were not to argue,' she said heatedly.

Robert expelled his breath noisily. 'All right, all right, I'm sorry. We don't seem capable of conducting a normal conversation, do we?'

'No.'

Julie walked slowly through an open doorway into a room to the right of the front door. Here the walls were all white apart from the fireplace wall which had been papered in deep blue damask. The fireplace was obsolete, of course, but an electric fire had been installed into the aperture to aid the central heating.

Robert followed her, leaving Emma to explore alone. 'This is your lounge,' he said, speaking formally. 'I realize the colour scheme might not be to your liking, but there was no time to wait for you to come and choose it for yourself. You can do it over later if you like.'

Julie tried to be equally formal. 'And have you chosen the furniture, too?'

Robert hesitated. 'No, actually Pamela did that.'

'That was kind of her.' Julie tried to think detachedly. 'Do you know what she's chosen?'

'Just the necessary things. You can choose your own ornamentation, pictures and so on later.'

'I see.' Julie walked to the windows which overlooked the front sweep of the house. 'And what do you call the necessary things?'

'Oh, carpets, a suite, television, and so on. I believe the carpet in here is going to be grey and blue, to match the wallpaper.' He shrugged. 'I believe the suite she chose was leather, but I can't be certain.'

'Thank you.'

Julie turned and walked out of the room again, crossing the hall to enter an almost identical room opposite. 'This is another reception room, I suppose.'

'That's up to you.' Robert entered the room and showed her how the central partition which divided this room from the one at the back of the house could be slid aside to reveal a dining area, ideal for if one wanted to give parties and needed more space.

Julie walked through. The garden at the back of the house

was extensive, and there were fruit trees and lawns which were presently being attended to by a gardener.

She could hear footsteps upstairs and guessed Emma was having the time of her life exploring. She opened a door which gave on to the hall again, and glanced at the other doors.

'You have a morning-room, or breakfast-room, just as you like, a large kitchen, and various outbuildings,' said Robert, noticing her questioning stare. 'Do you want to go upstairs?'

Julie's lips twitched. The tension between them was such that she felt if she didn't laugh she would burst into tears. Robert saw her amusement and frowned. 'Is something funny?'

Julie sobered, shaking her head. 'No,' she said quickly. 'No, of course not.'

Robert walked to the foot of the stairs. 'You can go alone, if you'd rather,' he said coldly, indicating that he was aware of what had caused her to smile.

Julie looked up at him and sighed. 'I'm sorry, Robert,' she said huskily. 'Just give me time. I – well, it's all so – so – different.'

Robert looked down at her intently. 'Do you think I'm not aware of that?' he demanded harshly.

Julie trembled for a moment in the grip of emotions she could not entirely control, and then without another word, she turned and hurried up the stairs to find Emma – and security.

CHAPTER FOUR

IT was almost two o'clock before they left the house. Emma had insisted on seeing everything, it was all new and exciting to her, and she had asked Robert dozens of questions, seemingly appointing him her adviser. Julie had accompanied them round with a bitter-sweet feeling of intrusion.

In one of the upstairs rooms they had discovered the trunks which had come by sea from Malaya, and Emma begged Julie to open them.

'But, darling, there's nowhere to put anything yet,' Julie had protested. Then: 'But perhaps we ought to take some of our clothes back to the apartment.' She looked up at Robert. 'How long – how much longer are we likely to be staying with you?'

Robert drew out a case of cigars and put one between his teeth. 'I'm told the house will be ready for occupation in about a week. That means you should be able to move in in – say ten days.'

'Ten days!' echoed Julie, in surprise. She opened her handbag to look for the keys of the trunks. 'Then we'll have to take some of these things. Emma and I can't continue to wear the same things day after day.'

Robert went down on his haunches beside the trunks, examining the padlocks. 'You could buy yourself some new clothes,' he remarked, without looking up.

Julie paused a moment. 'Could we? What with?'

Robert straightened. 'My mother has accounts at all the major stores in town. You can get anything you want and charge it.'

'No, thanks.' Julie continued to fumble about in the

bottom of her bag. 'Damn, where are they?'

Robert controlled his temper with apparent difficulty. 'Must you be so rude?' he snapped. 'You must know, as Michael's widow, you're entitled to anything you need.'

Julie's eyes sparkled with anger as she looked up. 'What? And have your mother tell me how dependent I am upon you?'

Robert's face darkened. 'One day, Julie . . .' he muttered menacingly, and taking a deep breath he went down on his haunches again beside the trunks.

Julie hid her nervousness at his words and a moment later produced the set of keys from her bag. Robert reached up and took them wordlessly from her hand, and after examining them he found the right key for the trunk nearest to him and unlocked it abruptly. Then he unfastened the leather straps which were a subsidiary means of support and lifted the heavy lid.

Emma jumped about excitedly, and would have delved into the trunk as soon as it was open had not Robert restrained her. Julie surveyed the packed contents with sudden emotion. Several newspaper-wrapped packages nestled among cotton sheets and bedcoverings, while the top of a cardboard box containing some china and glassware was just visible.

Gathering her composure, she shook her head, finding it difficult to articulate suddenly. 'I – this is the wrong one,' she said tautly. 'Our – our clothes are in the other.'

Robert closed the trunk lid again, much to Emma's disappointment, fastened the straps and secured the padlock. Then he pocketed the keys. Julie stared at him in surprise.

'Come along,' he said, 'That will do for now.'

Julie made a protesting gesture. 'But our clothes—'

Robert walked to the door of the room. 'Later,' he said.

Julie hunched her shoulders, and kicked one of the trunks

with the toe of her shoe. 'I've got to get some things,' she insisted.

Robert shook his head. 'You're not unpacking the trunks,' he stated unequivocally. 'Now, let's go. It's late, and I'm hungry.'

Julie hesitated a moment longer and then acquiesced. She didn't want to unpack the trunks, not now, and she couldn't help but feel a reluctant appreciation of his perception.

As they got into the car again, Robert said: 'We'll have lunch at the Black Bull in the village. I understand they do a very good grill. Does that appeal to you?'

Julie shrugged, settling into her seat. 'If you like.'

Robert's expression darkened, but he said nothing, merely flicked the ignition and set the powerful engine in motion.

The Black Bull was one of the pubs they had seen on their arrival. It was obviously quite well patronized at lunch time, for there were several cars parked on the forecourt and along the village green opposite.

The dining-room was not full, but the head waiter looked rather put out when they appeared. 'I'm afraid we stop serving lunches at a quarter to two,' he said, rather aggressively.

Julie sighed, but Robert seemed not a bit perturbed. 'I booked a table,' he explained calmly. 'My name's Pemberton.'

It was remarkable, thought Julie cynically, some three-quarters of an hour later, how that name could produce such a change in attitude. As she spooned a delicious concoction of strawberries and fresh cream into her mouth, she realized that the dining-room was deserted now and no doubt the catering staff were impatient to leave, too. And yet here they were, happily replete after a meal which even her failing appetite had been unable to resist. The steaks had been marvellous, the salad crisp and mouth-watering, the french fried potatoes hot and appetizing. Emma had eaten everything that had been put before her and was presently listening intently to Robert as he explained how strawberries could be grown in other parts of the world at different times of the year.

Robert looked up suddenly and caught her gaze upon them and a strange expression came into his eyes. 'Well?' he said. 'Did you enjoy it?'

Julie finished the wine in her glass and lay back in her chair. 'It was marvellous!' she exclaimed.

'Coffee?' he queried, but she shook her head.

'Don't you think we should go? I mean – obviously they're waiting to close.'

Robert half smiled. 'I shall see they don't lose by it.'

Julie bent her head. 'You think money buys anything, don't you?'

Robert's expression was grim suddenly. 'It bought you, didn't it?'

Julie looked up. 'What do you mean?'

Robert gave her a cynical look. 'You're not about to tell me you'd have married Michael if he'd been a penniless seaman, are you?'

Julie was horrified, and she glanced quickly at Emma, but she seemed unaware of their conversation, concentrating on the contents of her glass of Coke. 'I don't know what you mean.'

Robert rose abruptly to his feet. 'Oh, come off it, Julie. You weren't interested in Michael. You had plenty of opportunities to ditch me and marry him if that's what you'd wanted to do long before I left for Venezuela! No! It was me you wanted, so don't try to deny it!' His face was suddenly pale beneath his tan, and he turned savagely away and went in search of the head waiter, taking his wallet from his pocket as he went.

Julie shivered, and turning in her seat struggled to put on her coat. She would not have believed even Robert could be so cruel, and she felt physically sick.

By the time he returned, a smug gratified head waiter behind him, both Emma and Julie were ready and waiting, and Robert pulled on his sheepskin jacket before nodding briefly at the man and striding towards the door. Outside the cold air was revitalizing, and Julie breathed deeply before getting into the car.

The journey back to London was accomplished almost silently, even Emma seeming worn out by the morning's activities. After all, it had been only the day before that they arrived from Kuala Lumpur, and she had done well not to feel the effects more strongly than this. She had slept a good deal of the time though and consequently it was mostly a question of getting used to the time change.

Even so, her eyes were drooping by the time Robert brought the car to a halt outside the apartments, and Julie saw with some surprise that it was almost four o'clock and quite dark.

Emma brightened up in the lift and by the time they reached the apartment she was quite lively again. Lively enough to regale Lucy Pemberton with everything that had happened, including the problem of the trunks and the late lunch they had had at the Black Bull.

Robert disappeared almost immediately and Julie was left with her mother-in-law and daughter. Lucy listened attentively to what Emma had to say, almost as though she expected to hear something damning, thought Julie uncharitably, tugging off her coat and going towards the door which led to the hall. She intended putting her coat away and spending some time alone in her room. After the events of the last few hours she needed time to think.

But Lucy noticed her movements and said: 'Don't go, Julie. Halbird can put that away. Come and sit down. I want to hear what you think of the house.'

Julie threw her coat reluctantly over a chair and came to

57

take a chair near the others who were on the couch. Draping one leg over the arm of the soft leather armchair, Julie made a casual movement of her shoulders.

'It's very attractive. Have you seen it?'

'Oh, of course,' Lucy nodded. 'Pamela took me down there one day when we were on our way to visit her parents.'

Julie digested this. 'I see.'

'She found it, you know,' Lucy went on conversationally. 'Actually, it used to belong to some friends of her parents, but they were moving abroad – couldn't stand the climate, you know – and the house was going up for sale.'

Lucy's words stuck in Julie's throat. As she was sure they were intended to.

'Who's Pamela?' Emma was asking. 'Is she my auntie?'

Lucy turned to her smiling. 'She will be shortly, darling. She's going to marry Uncle Robert.'

'Oh!' Emma's lips made a round ring. 'Is she nice?'

'Very nice, darling. You'll be meeting her tomorrow.'

'Tomorrow? Will I? Why?' Emma was interested, her small chin supported by her fist.

Lucy glanced casually at her daughter-in-law. 'She and her parents are coming for dinner tomorrow evening. To meet you, Julie.'

'Are they?' Julie swallowed with difficulty. The idea of meeting the woman Robert was going to marry was not a pleasant one.

'Yes. Well, we thought we'd give you a couple of days to settle in, you know, before introducing you to our friends. And Saturday evening is as good a time as any, don't you think?'

'If you say so.' Julie found it difficult to be civil, and despised herself for feeling this way. Why should she immediately jump to the conclusion that Lucy was deliberately trying to antagonize her? Just because last night . . .

58

Determinedly, she said: 'I forgot to ask how you're feeling this morning.'

Lucy shrugged. 'I'm much better, thank you.' She turned back to Emma. 'Tell me, darling, did you see the swing in the garden of your new home? Hanging from the cherry tree? Pamela said she used to swing in it when she was a little girl.'

Emma shook her head wonderingly. 'No, I didn't.'

'I'm surprised at that.' Lucy frowned.

'We didn't go into the garden,' went on Emma honestly. 'Why didn't we, Mummy?'

Julie shrugged. 'There wasn't time, darling.'

'Nonsense!' Lucy sniffed. 'You had plenty of time.'

'Well, I suppose we didn't think of it,' said Julie, forcing herself not to get angry.

Lucy shook her head. 'You were long enough,' she said sharply.

Julie sighed. 'I'm sorry.'

'Did you bring nothing back with you, then?'

'No.' Julie swung her leg to the floor and stood up. 'It gets dark early, doesn't it?'

'Winter's drawing in.' Lucy raised her eyebrows. 'You'll find it very different from what you've been used to.'

'No doubt.' Julie's voice was terse.

Halbird came into the room at that moment. 'Can I bring you some afternoon tea, madam?' he inquired, looking at Lucy.

Lucy considered a moment. 'Oh, yes – yes, I suppose so.'

'Not for me,' said Julie, turning abruptly. 'I – er – I'm going to take a bath.'

'Yes, madam,' Halbird smiled.

'Where is Mr. Robert?' Lucy was speaking again.

'He's gone out, madam.'

'Gone out?' Lucy looked taken aback. 'But he's only just

got in.'

'Yes, madam.'

'Well? Did he say where he was going?'

'He said, if you asked, to tell you he has gone to the office, madam. He said he would be back shortly.'

'I see.' Lucy's nostrils flared.

'Can I watch television, Grandma?' Emma was wandering aimlessly about the room fiddling with anything she could lay her hands on.

Lucy looked irritated. 'I suppose you may,' she conceded reluctantly. 'Will you put it on, Halbird?'

'Yes, madam.' Halbird tuned the set and a few moments later colour pictures appeared. Emma was delighted.

'Oh, isn't it super?' she exclaimed of them all in general. Super was her favourite word at the moment.

Julie nodded and walked to the door.

'Would you like a tray of tea in your room, madam?' Halbird was addressing her this time.

Julie hesitated. 'I couldn't put you to the trouble,' she demurred.

Halbird shook his head. 'It's no trouble, madam.'

Lucy sighed with pointed boredom. 'If Mrs. Pemberton requires tea she can have it here with me, Halbird,' she said.

'Oh! Oh, yes, madam.' Halbird inclined his head politely, gave Julie a rather regretful stare, and left the room.

Julie opened the door, and Lucy turned her attention to her.

'I do hope you will not make a habit of embarrassing me in front of the servants, Julie,' she said sharply.

Julie sighed now. 'I'm sorry.'

'Are you?' Lucy looked sceptical, and taking out her handkerchief dabbed her nose ineffectually. 'Well, anyway, we've got to live together – for the next few days, at least – and I should be grateful if you could try and behave with less aggressiveness.'

Julie rested her forehead against the cool panels of the door. 'Very well,' she said. 'I'll try.'

Lucy thrust her handkerchief away. 'Will you be appearing for dinner this evening?'

'Of course,' Julie nodded.

'Very well.'

It was dismissal, and Julie resented it. But she closed the door with careful precision and made her way to her own room. Once there however she could not control her emotion, and she flung herself on the bed and allowed the hot tears to come.

Julie did not see Robert again until the afternoon of the following day.

He did not appear for dinner that evening and his mother took obvious pleasure in explaining that he and Pamela were attending a party at the home of some friends. He had apparently returned from his visit to the office while Julie was in the bath, and after bathing and changing himself he had gone straight out again. Emma, of course, went to bed about seven, so Julie and her mother-in-law dined alone.

It was a silent, uncomfortable meal, which Julie could not enjoy, and afterwards they watched television in the lounge.

'It will no doubt be very difficult for you to adapt yourself to our life here,' Lucy said, settling herself more comfortably in her chair. 'After all, you're not used to our ways, are you, Julie?'

Julie pretended an interest in the film they had been watching. 'What was that?' she asked absently, knowing perfectly well what Lucy had said.

'I said you'll find it difficult to adapt to our ways,' said Lucy sharply. 'I don't suppose life in an outpost in Malaya can be compared with social life here in London.'

'No, I don't suppose it can.' Julie tucked a strand of hair behind her ear.

'And you never had the opportunity to get used to us before Michael took you away,' went on her mother-in-law. 'I wouldn't have believed Michael could find fulfilment in such a place. He always seemed to enjoy his life here in London.'

'He joined the Navy long before he met me,' pointed out Julie shortly.

Lucy shrugged. 'Yes, I know. He always liked messing about in boats. Ever since he was a child. But to take an appointment overseas – a permanent appointment—'

'It was his idea.' Julie forced herself not to retaliate as Lucy expected her to do.

'I know. But so out of character.' Lucy reached for her glass of sherry. 'I expect it made things easier for you, though.'

Julie schooled herself to remain calm. 'Easier?' she echoed.

'Of course. I mean – well – Julie, you knew nothing of our ways, did you? You weren't used to entertaining – to arranging dinner parties! I don't suppose you'd ever composed a menu in your life, had you?'

'No. They didn't go in for that sort of thing much at the children's home,' Julie agreed shortly.

Lucy made a deprecatory little gesture. 'Now, Julie, don't let's quarrel again. I'm only trying to talk things over with you.'

'I'm not quarrelling,' retorted Julie, and then took a deep breath. 'It may come as some surprise to you to know, but Michael and I were happy – very happy!'

Lucy's eyes narrowed. 'Were you?'

'Yes, we were. He didn't care for your – your London season, whatever you call it! He did like messing about in boats, I agree with you there. We had a boat, just a small

62

one, and we spent most week-ends on it. We swam, we sunbathed. We entertained our friends. It was a – a wonderful life.'

Lucy's lip curled. 'Michael would still be alive today if you hadn't persuaded him to take that appointment.'

Julie paled. 'That's not true!'

'How do you know?' Lucy was openly antagonistic now.

Julie hesitated, compressing her lips. She didn't want to discuss the intimate details of Michael's health with this woman, even though she was his mother. But she had to be told. Sighing, she said: 'Because the reason he took the overseas appointment was that the doctor had told him he had to have a less active occupation.'

'What? I don't believe you!'

'It's true. I didn't know myself until – until after the second attack. The doctor had to explain.' Julie flung herself back in her chair. 'Michael refused to take his condition seriously.'

Lucy stared at her, her lips working, and for a moment Julie felt an intense feeling of compassion for her. 'You – you're making this up. He – he'd have told me. His own mother!'

Julie shrugged. 'You didn't know him as well as I did.'

'I knew him for twenty-eight years,' snapped Lucy contemptuously. 'Four or five times as long as you did.'

'Yes, but not as well as I knew him,' said Julie quietly. 'Believe me, I'm telling the truth, not trying to hurt you.'

Lucy rose from her chair. 'Have you told Robert this?'

Julie shook her head. 'No. I've told no one.'

'Then I wish you wouldn't,' said Lucy, moving restlessly about the room. 'I'd rather everyone thought of Michael's death as being one of those unexpected tragedies that sometimes occur.'

'So it was!' exclaimed Julie bitterly, realizing that Lucy

would not care for her friends to learn that Michael had hidden his illness from his family – from *her* – for more than six years.

'To you?' Lucy was asking now. 'Can you honestly say that?'

'Of course I can.' Julie was stung by her tone. The film on the television was meaningless to her now after the last few minutes.

Lucy made a dismissive gesture. 'Well, it's all in the past, isn't it? There's nothing either of us can do to bring him back.' Her lips tightened. 'Thank God, I still have Robert – and Emma, of course.'

Julie stood up. 'And when Robert gets married?' she said, unable to prevent herself from asking.

'What do you mean?'

Julie shook her head. 'Nothing.'

'You think that will make any difference to Robert?' Lucy was disdainful now. 'Oh, no! Robert's not like Michael. He would never do anything to hurt me. And the girl he's going to marry understands the relationship we have. Pamela is not selfish. She and I are the greatest friends.'

Julie heaved a sigh. There was a lot she could say. It would be painfully easy to make some cruel comment about girl-friends and wives being different people, but she kept her thoughts to herself. Instead, she walked over to the cocktail cabinet and said: 'Can I get you another sherry?'

'No, thank you.' Lucy turned to watch her pouring herself another gin and tonic. 'That's the third gin and tonic you've had this evening, isn't it?'

Julie raised the glass to her lips deliberately. 'Yes, it is. Do you mind?'

Lucy shrugged haughtily. 'I should have thought my meaning was obvious.'

'Robert can afford it,' returned Julie, with a tight smile.

'Money has nothing to do with it. You don't want to turn

into an alcoholic, do you, Julie?'

'Oh, for heaven's sake!' Julie swallowed the remainder of the spirit and put her glass down on the tray with heavy deliberation. Then she glanced at the masculine watch she was wearing. 'It's nine-thirty. Do you have any objections if I go to bed?'

Lucy sniffed. 'Not at all. It's obvious we have little in common.'

Julie moved towards the door, clenching her fists, refusing to be drawn yet again. But it was terribly difficult for her in the circumstances. Lucy was determined to put her firmly in her place, and so far she appeared to be succeeding. Except that she was unaware of Julie's own determination not to be intimidated, and that the victories she was winning now did not mean that the war was over.

The following afternoon, Lucy took Emma to the park. It was one of those wonderful days that November can unexpectedly produce, when the frost on the trees is turned to a diamond sparkle by the brilliance of the sun and the air is as clear and as fresh as wine.

Emma had asked her mother to accompany them, but Julie had declined. She had guessed that Lucy wanted to be alone with the child, and she was her grandmother after all.

Robert was out, too. He had gone out that morning before Julie was even up, and had rung Halbird during the morning to say he would not be in to lunch. So Julie had the apartment to herself, apart from the manservant, of course.

She was sitting in the lounge enjoying the momentary sense of freedom when the door bell pealed. Getting automatically to her feet, she was forestalled by the arrival of Halbird.

'I'll attend to it, Mrs. Pemberton,' he assured her with his usual courtesy, and Julie subsided on to the couch again.

Halbird went through the lobby and opened the outer

door. She heard the muffled sound of voices, Halbird's raised in obvious surprise, and then the sound of the door closing. Glancing round, she saw him entering the lounge with an armful of boxes and parcels.

'Good heavens!' she exclaimed, with a smile. 'What's going on?'

Halbird hesitated, still holding the packages. 'They're for you, Mrs. Pemberton,' he said. 'Where shall I put them? In your room?'

'For me?' echoed Julie disbelievingly. 'But – but I haven't ordered anything.'

'Well, that's what the delivery boy said,' said Halbird firmly.

'Are you sure they're not for – for Mr. Robert's mother?'

'No, madam. Mrs. *Julie* Pemberton, the boy said.'

Julie got to her feet. 'Well, you'd better put them down here, Halbird. Don't just stand there. I'll see what's inside, shall I?'

'If you wish, madam. Or would you like me to do it for you?' Halbird smiled and Julie warmed to his approval.

He dropped the parcels on to the couch where she had been sitting, and as he did so Julie noticed the name on the top of one of the boxes. She stiffened. It was the name of one of the most famous couturiers in London, and suddenly she knew what the parcels were.

'Thank you, I can manage,' she said, in a suddenly taut voice. Then realizing that Halbird was looking at her curiously, she added: 'I – well, these things are – are not for me.'

'But the delivery boy—'

'Yes, I know what he said. And he thought they were. But they're not.' She bit her lip. 'Just leave it, Halbird. I – I'll deal with it.'

'Yes, madam.'

Halbird went back to the kitchen with obvious reluctance and Julie heaved a sigh, standing staring at the heap of packages with impatient eyes. Who was responsible for this? Robert? Or the unknown Pamela? Whoever it was, they could have them back again. She wanted nothing from the Pembertons!

Even so, sitting in the lounge, constantly in the company of so many intriguing parcels, was disturbing. Her natural curiosity urged her to look inside the boxes, to see what they had chosen for her without her knowledge.

But she determined not to give in to herself. Turning her back on them, she seated herself in an armchair and picked up the newspaper she had been reading when the doorbell rang. But suddenly there was a slithering sound and one of the parcels which had been thrown so carelessly on to the couch dislodged itself from the pile and fell noisily on to the carpet. The unexpected disturbance startled her, and she looked round angrily.

The box was lying, half open, its contents spilling on to the apricot carpet. She didn't know what it was, but the colour of the material was exciting. It seemed to be several shades of purple, blue and green, blending together in cloth that was threaded with silver.

Making an impatient exclamation, she got up and went across to it, getting down on to her haunches and gathering the box and its contents together. The material was soft and clinging against her bare forearms and on impulse she dropped the box on to the couch and shook out the garment.

It was a caftan, long and straight, with wide sleeves and an upstanding collar before a dipping neckline. Holding it against herself, she realized it was probably her size, and the realization irritated her.

With careless fingers, she folded it back into its box and jammed on the lid. Then she pressed her lips together broodingly and looked at the other boxes.

But even as she was contemplating breaking her word to herself and opening them the outer door of the apartment opened and a moment later Robert Pemberton entered the room. He was wearing a dark thigh-length overcoat with a collar of dark fur, and as he unfastened this as he entered the room she saw the cream suede suit beneath.

He looked surprised to find her alone and glanced round questioningly, ignoring the parcels on the couch with annoying deliberation. 'Where is everyone?'

Julie took a deep breath. 'They're at the park.'

'I see.' Robert removed his coat and Halbird appeared to take it.

'Afternoon tea, sir?' he suggested.

Robert looked at Julie, but she shook her head and he shook his too. 'No, thanks, Halbird,' he replied. 'Later, perhaps. When Mrs. Pemberton returns.'

'Yes, sir.' Halbird withdrew and Julie moved away from the couch to the centre of the room, waiting for the moment when he would chose to mention his gesture.

However, Robert seemed determined not to mention them, flinging himself into an armchair and lighting a cigar with irritating indifference. Finally Julie could bear it no longer.

'Well?' she said. 'Why did you do it?'

Robert chose to be obtuse. 'Do what, Julie?'

Julie sighed. 'Buy these things!'

Robert's gaze flickered over the parcels. 'Did I do that?'

'Well, didn't you?' Julie was angry.

'What if I did?'

'Oh, stop it!' Julie clenched her fists. 'I told you – I didn't want anything from you.'

Robert raised his dark eyebrows. 'Well, I'm sorry to disappoint you, but I'm not responsible.'

Julie frowned. 'You're not? Then who—? *Not* your mother!'

Robert shrugged. 'Why not?'

Julie sought about for a reason. 'She – she wouldn't.'

'Well, I'm sorry to disappoint you yet again, but it was she.' Robert surveyed her appearance critically. 'I gather she thought your wardrobe was – well – inadequate.'

'Like hell she did!' Julie tugged fiercely at her hair. 'How dare she try to direct what I'm going to wear?' She grimaced. 'Oh, of course. Why didn't I think of it before? It's your dinner party this evening, isn't it? Is she afraid I might disgrace her? The poor relative!'

Robert's face hardened. 'Calm yourself, Julie! Stop acting like a spoilt child! If my mother chooses to buy you some clothes, the least you could be is grateful!'

'Why? Why should I be grateful? I didn't ask for anything.'

Robert rose to his feet, his expression contemptuous. 'You sicken me, do you know that?' he demanded coldly.

'Not half as much as you sicken me!' retaliated Julie childishly, but he ignored her outburst.

'You're determined to make things difficult, aren't you?' Robert stood looking down at her, his eyes mirroring his distaste.

Julie endeavoured to remain unmoved outwardly at least, but it was terribly difficult in the face of such hostility. 'If – if my clothes are not good enough for your – your friends, then I shall remain in my room this evening.'

Robert shook his head. 'You will do as I say.'

'Why should I?' Julie took a couple of steps back, half afraid of the anger she had aroused in him. 'You – your mother must have known how I would feel. That's probably why she did it.'

Robert raked his fingers through the thickness of his hair, resting his hand at the back of his neck almost wearily.

'Don't talk rubbish!' he exclaimed shortly. 'You know perfectly well that practically everything you wore out in Malaya will be unsuitable for this climate in winter.' He looked down at the pile of boxes. 'Haven't you looked at any of these?'

'No. I didn't even open the lids,' replied Julie defensively.

Robert hesitated a moment and then unbuttoning his jacket he bent and lifted the lid of the nearest box. Inside was a trouser suit of olive green tweed. He shook it out and regarded it critically. 'This should suit you very well,' he remarked, his voice controlled again.

Julie bent her head. 'You don't care how much you humiliate me, do you?' she asked, in a small voice.

At this, Robert straightened, dropping the trouser suit carelessly on to the couch. 'Why should I?' he asked harshly. 'You didn't mind humiliating me.'

Julie stared at him then, her green eyes wide, a pulse throbbing in her forehead. 'I – humiliated – you,' she echoed. 'How?'

Robert turned away, reaching for a cigar from the box on the low table nearby. Putting it between his teeth, he searched his pockets for his lighter. Then flicking it, he said: 'How did you think I'd feel when I came back and found you'd married Michael?'

Julie put a defensive hand to her throat. 'I'd rather not discuss it,' she said unevenly.

Robert's lips twisted. 'I'll bet you wouldn't. What can you say, after all? It's irrefutable!' A cruel smile tugged at the corners of his mouth. 'Oh, but you were good for me, Julie. Really good. You made me realize exactly what a bloody fool I'd been—'

'You don't understand!' Julie couldn't prevent the interjection.

'Oh, I understand perfectly, Julie. Half the attraction was

the money, after all, wasn't it? I'd slipped out of your net, and one bank balance was as good as another!'

Julie drew back her hand and her fingers stung across the lean muscles of his cheek, successfully silencing any further comment on his part. She didn't know what she expected then; some form of retaliation, she supposed. But Robert did nothing except hold her wavering gaze for a long penetrating moment, while the red marks of her fingers became visible on his face, and then he turned and walked abruptly out of the room.

Julie stared at the closed door with tear-glazed eyes. Oh, God, she thought nauseously, what have I done now?

She turned to the pile of boxes on the couch and had the absurdly childish notion to tear them and their contents to shreds. But that would prove nothing, except that she was indeed the adolescent he accused her of being.

Taking a deep breath, she gathered them together and making two journeys, she carried them all into her bedroom. Once there, she tumbled the contents on to the bed and found hangers to put them away in the wardrobes that lined one wall of the room. She didn't quite know what her motives were, but one thing was certain, these clothes would enable her to meet Lucy Pemberton on her own terms . . .

CHAPTER FIVE

THAT evening Julie took a long time preparing for dinner. Whatever else Pamela Hillingdon and her parents might say about her, it would not be that she had not taken care with her appearance.

Among the clothes which Lucy had had sent round for her inspection was a gown of turquoise velvet, soft and expensive, the hem edged with a pale fur which she suspected might be mink. The sleeves were long and full, the neckline low and round. It was a beautiful dress and it gave Julie's slender figure an added allure. Julie wondered, rather dryly, whether Lucy's efforts to make her daughter-in-law acceptable to her friends might not have repercussions of a different nature.

She had put up her hair this evening, leaving only tantalizing tendrils of silver silk to caress her cheeks and the nape of her neck. She knew she had never worn anything more becoming and the knowledge of her own attractiveness gave her confidence at a time when she most needed it.

As she walked along the hall later she heard the sound of voices from the lounge, and realized that Robert's guests had already arrived. She could hear Emma's voice, too. Lucy had suggested she be allowed to stay up to meet Robert's fiancée and Julie had had, perforce, to agree. But she had insisted that Emma put on her pyjamas and dressing gown and be ready for bed as soon as the introductions were over.

It took a great deal of courage to open the lounge doors and step into the room, and as she did so the talk in the room subsided and all eyes turned in her direction.

Lucy was the first to speak. Approaching her daughter-in-law, with a fixed smile on her face, she said: 'Oh, there you are, Julie! We've been waiting for you. Come and be introduced to everyone.'

Julie suffered Lucy to take her arm and draw her forward, her eyes going straight to the tall young woman standing beside Robert. Pamela Hillingdon was not at all as Julie had imagined, although there was no denying her attractiveness. Chestnut-haired, a full, almost voluptuous figure, her gown of cyclamen jersey moulding her body, she carried herself with supreme self-confidence, and Julie felt a little of her own confidence melting away beneath that patronizing gaze.

Her eyes flickered to Robert, dark and masculine in his dinner clothes, and she felt a tightening of her stomach muscles that made her feel slightly sick. His grey eyes were hidden beneath the thickness of his lashes, and his face was expressionless.

'Francis – Louise – this is my daughter-in-law, Julie. Julie, this is Pamela's father and mother. And Pamela, too. Darling, this is Julie!'

Julie shook hands automatically. Pamela's parents were younger than she had imagined they would be, probably just in their late forties, and Francis Hillingdon was regarding her with unconcealed admiration in his blue eyes. He was rather an attractive man, thought Julie detachedly. Not as tall as Robert, but sturdily built, with greying dark hair, and long sideburns.

Louise was like her daughter, tall and muscular, on eye level terms with her husband. They made Julie feel quite insignificant.

After the introductions were over, Francis said: 'We've just been introduced to your daughter, Julie. A charming young lady.' He grinned and Julie warmed to him.

Emma giggled. 'Mr. Hillingdon thought my pyjamas and dressing gown were a new style of evening dress.'

Julie smiled then. 'Did he? I hope you explained that young ladies have to get their beauty sleep.'

Emma wrinkled her nose. 'Do I have to go to bed?'

'You do indeed.' Julie was firm.

'What will you drink, Julie?' That was Robert, his voice cool and detached.

'Gin and tonic, please.' Julie refused to acknowledge Lucy's abrupt tightening of her lips.

'How are you settling down to life in England?' Pamela seemed to think it necessary to say something now that Robert had deserted her to get Julie's drink.

'I expect you find it rather cold, don't you?' Louise Hillingdon frowned. 'You were in Malaya, weren't you?'

'That's right.' Julie nodded. 'Oh – thank you.' She took her glass from Robert as he proffered it. 'Yes, it is quite cold. But the apartment is centrally heated, so I haven't noticed it much.'

'How do you like your house?' Francis offered her a cigarette which she accepted. 'It used to belong to some friends of ours.'

Julie bent to his lighter, steadying it with her hand, her lashes lifting so that she could thank him with her eyes. 'Yes, so I understand. And it seems very nice. Er – Robert took me to see it yesterday.'

Pamela glanced at her fiancé, stepping back a little so that he was included in their circle again. 'When will Julie be able to move in, darling?'

Robert put a cigar between his teeth. 'In a little over a week, I believe, Pamela. The decorators are almost finished.'

'Do you like the decorations?' Pamela was looking at Julie again.

Julie decided to be polite. 'Very much. You had some hand in them, I hear.'

Pamela smiled. 'Yes. It was quite fun. Sort of practice for

Rob and me when we find our own home.'

Julie didn't like the abbreviation of Robert's name, but it was nothing to do with her, and in any case Lucy chose that moment to say:

'Aren't we silly, standing here? We could all be sitting comfortably.'

Robert turned. 'Will you come and sit down, Louise?' he inquired of his mother-in-law-to-be.

Louise sipped the remainder of her sherry and then putting down her glass she drew the skirts of her black gown about her and accepted the chair he offered. Francis stood back, indicating that Julie should precede him and as Pamela was already subsiding on to the couch, Julie took an armchair. To her surprise, Francis took the chair beside her leaving Lucy to sit with Louise.

Emma perched on the arm of Julie's chair, and conversation became general. But after a few minutes, Julie realized her daughter was drooping, her lids dropping over her eyes with tiredness. Standing up again, she said: 'Come along, darling. I'll put you to bed.'

Both Robert and Francis had risen too and with an apologetic smile Julie told Emma to say goodnight to her grandmother and the others and hurry along to her room.

By the time Julie returned to the lounge, dinner was ready, and they all went through to the dining room. Robert and Lucy sat at either end of the table with Pamela and her father on one side, and Julie and Louise Hillingdon on the other.

As usual the meal was delicious. The main course was roast duckling, one of Julie's favourites, but as she wasn't relaxed she couldn't enjoy it. However, Francis Hillingdon put himself out to be as entertaining as possible and she found herself laughing quite helplessly at him at times as he described a trip he had made recently to central Africa. His descriptions of his experiences at the airport in Nairobi brought a smile even to Robert's brooding countenance and by the time they adjourned to the lounge for coffee Julie had decided she liked him enormously. He was so friendly, so uncomplicated; and while neither Pamela nor her mother had been at all hostile, there was nevertheless a certain reserve about their reception of her which made Julie wonder exactly what they had been told.

In the lounge, Robert put several long-playing records on the hi-fi equipment, and presently the room was filled with the fourth dimensional quality of Burt Bacharach's music. Drinks were offered and Julie accepted another gin and tonic. The wine they had drunk with the meal had made her comfortably mellow, and she no longer felt the automatic tightening of her stomach muscles every time she looked at Robert.

Pamela and he were sharing a couch, while Louise and Lucy seemed to find plenty to talk about. Naturally as they both shared the distinction of being the mothers of the prospective bride and groom there was always the wedding to discuss, so that Julie found herself left with Francis.

Not that she minded. Of them all, Francis was the easiest to talk to, and they sat together discussing books they had read, and as Julie had been away from London for so long Francis was quite willing to bring her cultural knowledge up to date. From time to time, Julie was conscious of Robert's brooding gaze upon her, but she refused to meet his eyes and read the censure she knew she would find there.

By the time the Hillingdons left Julie felt as though she had known Francis for years and she was grateful to him for making an evening which could have been difficult pass so quickly and enjoyably.

Robert accompanied them down to their car, and after the door was closed Lucy sighed with some satisfaction. 'Aren't they a charming family?' she asked of Julie, obviously feeling pleased with herself.

'I hardly spoke to anyone except Francis,' replied Julie, flinging herself carelessly into a chair.

'*Francis!*' Lucy was obviously horrified. 'I hope you didn't call him that.'

'Why not?' Julie frowned.

'Well, my dear, it's just not done. Do you know who he is?'

Julie gave a resigned gesture. 'I don't particularly care.'

'Then perhaps you should. He's the head of the Hillingdon Corporation. His father is Sir Arnold Hillingdon. Pamela's father will inherit the title on his death.'

'Big deal!' Julie was unimpressed.

Lucy's cheeks paled a little with annoyance. 'I might have known that that information would mean little to you. Anyway, it doesn't matter. I doubt whether you'll be seeing much of them. And after you move to Thorpe Hulme...'

'Oh, yes, I know. I'll be out of the way,' remarked Julie bitterly.

Lucy emptied a brimming ashtray into a waste bin. 'I didn't know you smoked.'

'I don't.'

'But you did this evening.'

'Social smoking, that's all.' Julie sighed. 'Can I go to bed?'

Lucy turned. 'Why not?'

'I wasn't sure whether I had permission or not.' Julie was sardonic.

The outer door of the apartment suddenly opened and closed again to admit Robert. He came into the room unbuttoning his dinner jacket and wrinkling his nose at the pall of cigarette smoke. Suddenly, he looked exactly like Emma – she wrinkled her nose, too, and Julie caught her breath.

She was conscious of him coming to stand before her chair. 'Well?' he challenged coldly. 'I see you changed your mind.'

Julie did not reply. She knew he was referring to her clothes. But Lucy was puzzled.

'Changed her mind about what?'

Robert made a gesture. 'Nothing. Forget it!' He glanced round the room. 'What a mess!'

There were ashtrays overflowing on to table tops, empty glasses strewn around, the sleeves of several records tipped aimlessly against chair legs, dishes of nuts and potato chips looking lost and unappetizing in the general disarray.

Lucy shrugged. 'Halbird will soon deal with it in the morning,' she said.

'No doubt.' Robert went to the cabinet to pour himself some Scotch. 'Do you want another drink?' He was looking at his mother, but Julie chose to reply.

'Yes, please,' she said deliberately. 'You know what I like.'

Robert made no comment, but he poured a gin and tonic and brought it across to her.

'You drink too much!' said Lucy sharply, unable to hide her impatience.

'But not in company,' drawled Julie deliberately. 'I didn't let you down this evening, did I?'

'That will do!' Robert swallowed his Scotch at a gulp.

'The sooner Julie and I put some distance between us the better,' retorted his mother angrily.

Robert regarded her moodily. 'No one's stopping you from returning to your own apartment,' he stated.

Julie blinked. It was not like Robert to answer his mother in such an offensive tone.

'What?' Lucy was saying now in a horrified way. 'And leave you here alone – *with her*?'

'Why not?' Robert's expression was ironic. 'Surely you don't imagine it would matter, one way or the other.'

'Of – of course it would matter.' Lucy stared at him, trying to read his mind. 'Besides, I doubt whether Pamela would like me to leave.'

Robert ran a hand round the back of his neck. 'Why not?'

Lucy sniffed resentfully. 'Don't be obtuse, Robert.'

'I'm not being obtuse, Mother. If you mean what I think you mean you don't honestly suppose that if I wanted to climb into bed with Julie your presence in the apartment would make the slightest bit of difference!'

'Robert!' Lucy was pale.

He gave an impatient ejaculation. 'It's the truth, Mother.' His lips twisted. 'The fact of the matter is that your presence here as a chaperon is unnecessary. Julie was my brother's wife – therefore I shall provide for her. But that's all. Satisfied?' He turned away. 'Now I suggest we all go to bed. I'm tired.'

Julie stood up, finishing her gin and tonic as she did so. Swaying slightly, she regarded them both bitterly. 'You put that so charmingly, Robert,' she remarked sarcastically. 'Might I add that whether or not you choose to provide for *me* is entirely up to you!' And dropping her glass noisily on to a side table she inclined her head regally and left the room.

The next few days passed comparatively uneventfully. Needless to say, Lucy did not return to her own apartment, as Julie had known she wouldn't, but as they both avoided one another there were few opportunities for open confrontation.

They saw little of Robert, and if Emma thought this was a strange household she had been brought to, the excitement of trips about London with either Julie or her grandmother was more than enough to distact her.

In other circumstances, Julie would have asked Robert whether she might visit the offices of the Pemberton Company. Her old boss, Vincent Harvey, still worked there so far as she knew, and it would have been nice to renew her acquaintance with him again.

But Robert's attitude encouraged little except antagonism, and a painful kind of acceptance inside her, and although he went frequently to the skyscraper building in Spanish Mews, she was not invited.

One morning, when Julie had been back in England for almost a week, the telephone rang and as she was alone in the apartment at the time she answered it. To her surprise it was Francis Hillingdon.

'Julie?' he exclaimed.

'That's right.' Julie moved the telephone receiver from one hand to the other. 'Is that – is that Mr. Hillingdon?'

'Francis,' he amended dryly. 'Mr. Hillingdon sounds as though you consider me an old man.'

Julie smiled. 'I didn't mean that at all.'

'No, I'm sure you didn't.' Francis sounded amused. 'Are you well?'

'Fine, thank you.' Julie glanced behind her, realizing Halbird had come to the door of the lounge. 'Er – who did you want to speak to? I'm afraid Robert's at the office and my mother-in-law has taken Emma to the Zoo.'

'I wanted to speak to you, Julie,' Francis stated surprisingly, and Julie shrugged helplessly at Halbird.

'You wanted to speak to me?' she repeated, for the manservant's benefit, and Halbird nodded politely and withdrew.

'That's right. I wanted to ask if you were free for lunch today.'

'For lunch?' Julie gathered her thoughts. She was repeating his words parrot-fashion and she was beginning to sound ridiculous. 'But – why?'

Francis laughed. 'Do I have to give a reason? Can't you just accept that I want to have lunch with you?'

Julie was taken aback. 'Well, I don't know—' she

began.

'Why? On your own admission Robert is at the office and Lucy and Emma are at the Zoo. What's stopping you? Unless you have a prior engagement, of course, in which case I'll offer suitable regrets and ring off.'

Julie sighed. 'It's so unexpected, that's all.'

'Well?' Francis waited.

Julie bit her lower lip, a mass of conflicting emotions. The idea of having lunch with Francis was attractive. He was an amusing and interesting man, and she had no doubt that she would enjoy herself. But there were other things to be considered: what Robert might think, to begin with, and what malicious construction Lucy might place on the whole affair.

But as though her mother-in-law's petty restrictions were a kind of driving exhortation to commit the unforgivable crime of disobedience, Julie made a decision.

'All right,' she agreed. 'I'd love to have lunch with you. Where shall we meet?'

Francis sounded delighted. 'I'll pick you up at the apartment,' he suggested. 'About twelve?'

Julie ran her tongue over her lips. 'All right. But downstairs. I – I'll come down to meet you.'

'Fine.'

Francis rang off and Julie replaced her receiver with some trepidation. Well, she was committed now, and there was nothing she could do about it even if she wanted to. She had no idea where to contact Francis and in exactly one hour he would be downstairs waiting for her.

A thrill of excitement coursed along her veins. It was a long time since any man other than Michael had offered her a meal, and she went swiftly through to the kitchen to tell Halbird that she would not be in to lunch. He didn't ask with whom she was lunching, but she felt he thought she ought to have told him. However, she had no desire to arouse Robert's anger unnecessarily, and it was quite possible that she would be back before anyone knew she was gone. It wasn't until she was having a shower that she had to accept that by anticipating Robert's anger she was admitting that what she was about to do was wrong.

But why should it be? she asked herself fiercely, as she pulled on sheer tights over her shapely legs. After all, having lunch with a man was innocent enough.

She dressed in the green tweed trouser suit which Robert had considered would suit her. And it did. The dull colour was a perfect foil for the silvery brilliance of her hair which had been bleached whiter than normal by the hot Malayan sun. She left her hair loose, and she looked absurdly youthful as she went down in the lift at a minute past twelve.

Francis was leaning against the bonnet of his car parked outside under the eye of Norris, the commissionaire. However, when Norris saw Julie coming out of the building he raised his hand in polite acknowledgement. Julie smiled in return and ran the remaining few yards to where Francis was waiting.

It was a bitterly cold morning and there were traces of fog still hanging about. Julie half wished she had put on her fur coat over the trouser suit, but inside Francis's sleek Mercedes it was beautifully warm.

'That man thought I was a conspirator, I know he did,' remarked Francis with mock relief, sliding into the car beside her.

'He does take his duties rather seriously,' agreed Julie, laughing, her cheeks pink with the cold.

Francis regarded her intently for a long moment and then when she was beginning to feel self-conscious he turned and started the engine. 'You look pretty good,' he commented, concentrating on entering the stream of traffic in Eaton Gate. 'I wondered if you'd have second thoughts.'

Julie looked at him out of the corners of her eyes. 'Should

I have?'

Francis swung the wheel and the car moved swiftly towards the King's Road. 'Not from my point of view,' he replied.

'That's good.' Julie looked out of the car's windows. 'Where are we going?'

'I thought we might go to the Purple Pheasant,' he said, glancing in her direction for a moment to ascertain her interest. 'It's on the Slough Road. Heard of it?'

Julie shook her head. 'But that's not surprising in the circumstances,' she said, sighing. 'After all, it's six years since anyone invited me for lunch in England.'

Francis smiled. 'Then I shall consider myself honoured,' he remarked lightly. 'We'll have champagne, to celebrate.'

Julie laughed. It was very easy to be relaxed with Francis.

The Purple Pheasant deserved its excellent reputation. The meal was delicious, and the champagne Francis insisted upon heady and exciting. Altogether it was a delightful outing and Julie was sorry when it was over and they drove back to town.

The conversation throughout the meal had been light and inconsequential, but as they neared the apartment, Francis said:

'Will you come out with me again, Julie?'

Julie looked at his profile as he kept his eyes firmly on the traffic ahead of them. 'Do you want me to?'

'Of course.' His tone was serious now.

Julie bent her head. 'I don't know whether we should.'

'Why?' Francis took a moment to look at her. 'You've enjoyed it, haven't you?'

'Yes. But that's not the point, is it?'

'I don't understand.'

'Yes, you do, Francis. When – when you asked me out to

lunch, I asked you why, and you said – did there have to be a reason? Well, now there does.'

He frowned. 'Surely my reasons are obvious. I enjoy your company.'

'And your wife?'

'Louise? What about her?'

'Does she know you've taken me out today?'

'Why should she? It's nothing to do with her.'

'But it is.' Julie sighed. 'Can't you see what I'm getting at? If she finds out that we've been out and you've not told her – what is she going to think?'

Francis's expression was grim. 'Frankly, I couldn't care less.'

Julie stared at him. 'Why?'

The car was turning into the forecourt of the apartment building now and Francis brought it to a halt before replying. Then he turned sideways in his seat, his arm along the back of hers. 'Need I elucidate?' he asked softly. 'Our relationship has been on the rocks for years. Oh, we're still married, we still go through the motions of being a happily married couple for the sake of Pamela, and my parents. But that's all.'

Julie took a deep breath. 'I see.' She wished she had known this before accepting Francis's invitation. This changed things, changed them a lot.

Francis bent his head to regard the buttons of his jacket. 'That puts me beyond the pale, of course.'

'What do you mean?'

Francis looked up, his expression wry. 'Am I right in thinking that you're regretting going out with me now? You think – hell, I've got to walk warily here. This man's out for something more than just a friendly relationship!'

Julie coloured, and Francis swung round in his seat abruptly. 'You see,' he said. 'I'm right, aren't I?'

'And are you?' she asked softly.

'Am I what?'

'Out for more than a friendly relationship?'

Francis sighed. 'I'd be a fool and a liar to say no,' he replied briefly. 'But if you think that I'd ever force you to do anything you didn't want to do, you're mistaken. I like you, you attract me, I can't deny that either. But if all you want is my friendship, then I'm quite prepared to offer it.'

'Oh, Francis!' Julie stared at him helplessly.

'We've got very intense all of a sudden, haven't we?' he remarked lightly. 'This will never do.' He glanced at his watch. 'And I must go. I have an appointment – let me see – half an hour ago!'

Julie gasped. 'Half an hour ago! But you're late!'

'Hmm.' Francis didn't sound at all disturbed by the news.

'I'd better go.' Julie thrust open the car door and slid out, and Francis got out too and came round to her side of the vehicle.

'Well?' he said. 'Thank you for joining me.'

'Thank you!' Julie shook her head. 'It was marvellous.'

Francis nodded. 'Good.' He turned back to the car, but she stayed him with her hand.

'Aren't – aren't you going to invite me out again?'

Francis's eyes narrowed. 'You'd come?'

'As a friend, yes.'

Francis took her hand in both of his. 'All right. I'll ring you in a few days, if I may.'

Julie nodded. 'Do that. Goodbye, Francis.'

'Goodbye, Julie.' He nodded, allowed her hand to fall to her side and walked swiftly round to climb into his car.

Going up in the lift Julie pondered her motives for doing what she had just done. But there had been an enormous weight of unhappiness in Francis's eyes when he had told her so indifferently of his affairs. And he had not tried to pretend that he wanted a platonic relationship. That had really decided her, although she knew that was all they could ever have. That, and the fact that she knew how easy it was to be misunderstood in the most destructive circumstances.

CHAPTER SIX

WHEN Julie let herself into the apartment a few minutes later she could hear the sound of a feminine voice and her heart sank. Lucy was obviously back and no doubt would expect some explanation as to why Julie should have gone out without leaving any information where she might be.

Straightening the jacket of her suit, she dropped her handbag on to the table in the lobby and pushed open the lounge door. But it was not her mother-in-law who was seated on the couch and who turned to regard her curiously as she entered the room but a strange young woman. Robert was there, too, standing sombrely beside the long windows, his hands behind his back.

Julie closed the door and leaned back against it, her dark brows drawing together in puzzled expectation. Then her eyes flickered questioningly to her brother-in-law and he walked slowly across to stand behind the couch.

'Good afternoon, Julie,' he greeted her coldly. 'I'm so glad you've decided to return at last. Miss Lawson and I have been waiting for you for almost an hour.'

Julie moved away from the door, aware that Robert's cold words were merely the tip of the iceberg, so far as his anger was concerned. Had they been alone she was quite sure he would have taken hold of her and demanded forcibly to know where she had been. Or perhaps he already knew. Perhaps he had seen her arrive back with Francis.

She endeavoured to remain composed for Miss Lawson's sake, whoever she might be, and made a confused gesture. 'Yes?' she queried. 'Forgive me, but why have you been waiting for me?'

Robert's control was magnificent, but his eyes burned

with something much more malevolent than mere irritation at her absence. 'Miss Lawson is the governess I have employed for Emma,' he stated, his eyes holding hers almost against her will so that Julie felt a shaft of pure unadulterated fear inside her. 'You may recall, I mentioned the matter to you.'

She dragged her gaze away and tried to concentrate her attention on the young woman seated so relaxedly on the couch. She was not a decorative young woman, but the clever use of clothes and make-up had given her an attractive appearance, enhanced by her cap of auburn hair. She was regarding Julie with an appraising stare that was nothing short of insolent and Julie felt a fleeting sensation of annoyance. Then she firmly decided she was allowing Robert's attitude to influence her judgement. In a friendly fashion, she said: 'I'm sorry I wasn't here to welcome you, Miss Lawson.' She went towards her holding out her hand and the young woman took it languidly. 'I'm Julie Pemberton, Emma's mother.'

Miss Lawson decided it was time to show some enthusiasm and rose to her feet. She was taller than Julie, and this seemed to please her. 'How do you do, Mrs. Pemberton,' she said politely. 'I'm pleased to make your acquaintance. Tell me, where's Emma?'

Julie raised her eyes to Robert's reluctantly. 'Haven't they come back yet?' she asked, almost unnecessarily. 'Your mother has taken Emma to the Zoo.'

Robert folded his arms across his chest. He looked bigger and more powerful than ever after Francis's shorter, less muscular frame. 'It isn't necessary for Miss Lawson to meet Emma today. My main concern in arranging this meeting was to enable you to meet Miss Lawson and hear her suggestions regarding Emma's schooling.'

Julie took a deep breath. 'I wasn't aware that we had made any definite decision regarding Emma's schooling,' she remarked, with assumed nonchalance.

Robert's expression darkened. 'On the contrary, it's all arranged. Miss Lawson will take up residence with you at Thorpe Hulme at the end of the week when you move in. I can see no difficulties whatsoever.'

Julie held up her head. She would not be intimidated in front of this strange young woman. 'I'm not at all convinced that Emma requires a governess,' she said firmly. 'I'm sure the school in the village will be more than adequate to deal with her early education. When she's a little older—'

Robert's eyes glittered. 'Allow me to be the best judge of that, Julie,' he said dourly.

'I think we should discuss it a little more,' she said, trying to be conciliatory.

'There's nothing to discuss.'

'I don't agree.' Julie gave Miss Lawson a faint smile. 'I've no doubt that Miss Lawson is an exceptionally good governess, but I should prefer Emma to mix with other children during the day.'

'I do not intend to conduct an argument with you, Julie.' Robert's arms fell to his sides. 'As I've said, I brought Miss Lawson here so that you should get to know one another.'

Julie seethed, but she turned to the girl helplessly. 'Have you had some tea, Miss Lawson? Would you like some?'

'Thank you.' Miss Lawson inclined her head coolly and Julie walked quickly across the room to the door, indicating that the governess should be seated again. In the hall between the lounge and the kitchen, Robert caught up with her, preventing her progress by grasping her wrist in a vice-like hold.

'One minute!' he snarled savagely. 'Where the hell do you think you've been until this time? Do you realize it's after half past three?'

Julie stared up at him indignantly. The hall was narrow at this point and his hold on her wrist brought her closer to him than she had been since she returned from Malaya. His fingers on her wrist were cool and hard, but the anger she could see so clearly in his eyes was anything but cool. He was blazing.

'You're not my keeper, Robert,' she said clearly.

'I didn't say I was. I asked where you had been.'

'I went out for lunch.'

'Damn you, I know that. I want to know with whom?' Robert's finger tightened. 'Do you want me to break your wrist?'

'You wouldn't dare!'

'Try me!' Robert's burning eyes gave an indication of his determination.

Julie's throat felt constricted. 'You – you brute!' She almost spat the words at him. 'If you must know, I went to lunch with Francis!'

'Francis?' Robert shook his head. 'Francis who?'

'Francis Hillingdon. Now will you please let go of my wrist?'

'Francis Hillingdon!' Robert was obviously astounded, but still he did not let go of her. 'Pamela's father?'

'The very same,' retorted Julie sarcastically. 'Let me go!'

Robert ignored her demand. 'What the hell are you doing having lunch with him? You hardly know him.'

'Well, I know him a little better now,' returned Julie, in a taunting voice, unable to prevent the jibe.

'You bitch!' Robert stared down at her upturned face with a twisted expression on his. 'How did you come to have lunch with Francis?'

'He asked me,' answered Julie, grimacing. 'What's it to you? There was no harm in it. He rang me this morning and asked me to lunch. That's all.'

Robert's eyes narrowed. 'I didn't know Francis went in for that kind of thing.'

'He doesn't. And what do you mean – that kind of thing? I've told you. It was perfectly innocent.'

'I bet.' Robert looked down at the slender wrist in his grasp. 'I could snap this as easily as a matchstick,' he remarked grimly. 'Or perhaps it's your neck I should break!'

Julie gave a nervous laugh, unaccountably apprehensive of the look in his grey eyes. 'Now stop it, Robert. We – we're wasting time. Miss – er – Miss Lawson will be wondering what's happened to her tea.'

'I don't give a damn about Miss Lawson's tea!' snapped Robert harshly.

'Well, I do.' Julie struggled unsuccessfully to free herself, and in the struggle a couple of the buttons of her suit jacket came unfastened so that she drew the gap together self-consciously.

Robert's eyes were disturbingly insolent. 'Have you got anything on under that jacket?' he demanded thickly.

Julie's cheeks went scarlet. 'Robert, please,' she pleaded uneasily, but he took no notice.

Suddenly, he pulled her closer to him, twisting her wrist behind his back, so that her body was pressing against the hard, muscular length of his. Then he looked at her, his eyes half closed.

'Well?' he muttered huskily. 'What are you going to do now?'

Julie wriggled impotently beneath that devastating gaze, but her movements only served to incite him further and his hand on her wrist tightened, pressing her so closely against him she felt she couldn't breathe.

'Robert, please,' she said again, but faintly now, her senses becoming unwillingly inflamed by the pure sensuality of him. The clean, male smell of him was in her nostrils, the heat of his body was invading hers. He slid his free hand over her shoulder and under the heavy weight of her hair, cupping her nape, tipping back her head so that she was forced to look into his tormented face.

'Tell me,' he muttered grimly, so that she became convinced he was trying to torture himself more than her. 'Tell me, Julie, how did it feel being married to Michael? How could you let him touch you? How could you lie in his arms, and let him make love to you knowing that you didn't love him?'

Julie tried to turn her head from side to side, but her face was pressed against his chest and she could scarcely breathe. Releasing her jacket, she put her hand against his chest in an effort to push him away from her, but instead her fingers encountered the soft silk of his shirt and lingered. On impulse, she slid two fingers between the buttons and touched the hair-roughened skin beneath.

'Dear God,' she heard him groan, and then he bent his head and his mouth fastened on hers, parting her lips with savage insistence. His kiss was brutal, violent, passionate, and yet contemptuous, but for all that when he would have lifted his head, she gripped a handful of his hair, clinging to him so that instead of letting her go he slid his arms around her, beneath the offending jacket against the warm skin of her midriff. The kiss became deeper, hungrier, more demandingly intimate, so that Julie's bones turned to water and she felt weak and helpless. Only Robert had ever had the power to reduce her resistance to nil.

When at last he let her go, she swayed a little, unable to orientate herself immediately. Robert was pale, scrubbing the back of his hand across his mouth bitterly, his expression more forbidding than ever.

'You selfish little bitch!' he bit out savagely. 'You don't change a bit, do you? You don't care who you hurt!'

Julie buttoned her jacket with trembling fingers, her momentary weakness vanishing beneath the tide of his anger. 'I didn't ask you to touch me!' she exclaimed defensively, aware that so far as he was concerned her actions had only damned her still further in his eyes.

Robert raked a hand through his hair, his face contorted. 'No,' he conceded grimly. 'You didn't do that. But you're not going to try and tell me you objected, are you?'

Julie assumed a nonchalance she was far from feeling. 'No, I shan't contradict you, Robert,' she replied, with feeling. 'Why should I? You wouldn't believe me anyway, and besides, you always were an expert at making love, weren't you? How did you gain your experience, I wonder?'

Robert's jaw tightened and a muscle worked in his cheek. He stood looking at her for a long disturbing moment, and then, without another word, he pushed past her, disappearing into his own room. Julie stood where he had left her, realizing she was trembling all over. Then, with determination, she approached the door of the kitchen and putting her head round it, said, in an amazingly calm tone: 'Could we have tea for three, please, Halbird?'

Julie would have liked to have gone to her room before re-entering the lounge, but Miss Lawson had been left alone long enough and she did not want to arouse suspicions from that quarter. Even so, she was intensely conscious of the fact that her cheeks were burning now and that her mouth must be bare of all lipstick. For an insane moment an intense longing to go to Robert's room slid over her, and then she forced herself to be sensible. That she still disturbed him physically was obvious, but that was not love, and while she might be capable of arousing a further exhibition of his sexual expertise, his eventual reactions would be the same. While she ...

Miss Lawson was sitting on the couch, smoking a cigarette, and she looked up rather impatiently as Julie entered the room.

'Oh, I'm – er – sorry for the delay, yet again,' murmured Julie inadequately. 'I – I've ordered some tea. Won't you tell me a little about yourself while we wait?'

The young woman regarded her in a hostile fashion which Julie didn't altogether understand. 'Do I take it I am to be Emma's governess, then?' she asked pointedly.

Julie seated herself opposite the girl on a matching couch of soft leather. 'Let us say, for the moment, I accept the status quo,' she said carefully.

Miss Lawson raised her eyebrows. 'But Mr. Pemberton is my employer, isn't he?'

'Indirectly, yes.' Julie sighed. 'Look, Miss Lawson, you and I are expected to live together. I don't think it's unreasonable that we should at least try to get to know one another, do you?' Trying to introduce a friendlier note, she went on: 'Now – what's your name, your Christian name? I can't call you Miss Lawson all the time.'

'It's Sandra, actually,' replied the girl. 'But I'd prefer to remain Miss Lawson in front of Emma. Familiarity is not good for discipline, you know.'

Julie tried to prevent the smile from disappearing from her face entirely. 'I don't think you'll require a great deal of discipline with a five-year-old, Miss – er – Sandra. Besides, Emma is not that kind of child.'

'What kind of child, Mrs. Pemberton?'

'The kind that continually requires discipline. Emma is a rather self-contained and self-controlled person. I can't honestly imagine her causing any great problem.'

'You're her mother, Mrs. Pemberton. You wouldn't understand the problems a teacher can come up against.'

'I should imagine it would depend a lot upon the teacher,' retorted Julie, getting quite heated in spite of herself.

Halbird broke up the atmosphere by wheeling in the tea trolley and for a while they were engrossed in plying cups of tea and plates of sandwiches. Julie had charge of the teapot, but she ate nothing. The idea of food at this moment was repugnant to her.

Sandra Lawson made a good meal. She ate heartily, and Julie thought rather uncharitably that if she wasn't careful she would run to fat. Only her height saved her from being overweight at the moment. She was drinking her third cup of tea when Robert reappeared.

He had changed, Julie saw at once, and from the drops of water glinting on his dark hair, he had had a shower too. In casual clothes he had a lazy indolence and Julie found it hard to believe that only a few minutes ago he had lost control of himself and made passionate love to her. How could he switch his emotions off like that, while she was still a quaking mass of nerves and sensations?

Sandra Lawson seemed pleased to see him. She smiled warmly in his direction and although the muscles of Robert's face scarcely relaxed at all, there was a faint softening in his expression as he looked towards her.

He looked at Julie, and his demeanour underwent a dramatic change. 'Well?' he asked curtly. 'Is everything arranged?'

Julie shrugged. 'Do I have any say in the matter?'

'*Julie!*' His tone was savage, and she realized he was not as indifferent as he appeared.

Julie shivered. 'Oh, very well. Make whatever arrangements you like.' She slid off the couch. 'My presence seems entirely incidental.'

Robert looked at her as though he would have liked to have said something more, but he seemed to change his mind and the sound of the outer door opening caused him to glance round rather irritably.

Emma bounded into the room, small and dark and utterly adorable in her red anorak and green trews. She stopped short at the sight of Sandra Lawson, and looked inquiringly towards her mother.

Julie bent down and hugged her. 'Hello, darling,' she said. 'Had a good day?'

'Oh! It was super, Mummy!' Emma was enthusiastic. Releasing herself from her mother, she skipped across to Robert, taking his hand in both of hers and tugging it excitedly. 'We saw absolutely everything, Uncle Robert, and Grandma bought me some ice cream and some Coke and heaps of sweets.'

'Did she indeed?' Robert's tone was dry, but the tenseness of his expression disappeared in the face of Emma's enchanting personality. There was no doubting the affection he had for her, and Julie wondered why the knowledge hurt so much.

'We saw some ponies, too,' went on Emma eagerly, 'and do you know what Grandma said? She said I might have a pony when we move to the country. Will I? Will you buy me one, Uncle Robert!'

'Emma!' Julie was annoyed, and Lucy, coming into the room at that moment folding her gloves into her handbag, said:

'Not now, Emma, not now!' rather irritably.

Then she saw Sandra Lawson and her expression became welcoming. 'Sandra! Sandra, my dear. I didn't know you were coming here today or I'd have made a point of being at home.'

'Miss Lawson wasn't aware of the arrangement herself until I rang her this morning,' remarked Robert, in explanation, helping Emma off with her anorak. He looked down at the child. 'Miss Lawson is to be your governess. Do you know what a governess is?'

Emma frowned. 'Is it like an *ayah*?' she asked.

Robert shook his head. 'No, an *ayah* is a sort of nanny. A governess is like a teacher. She teaches you lessons.'

Emma's small face grew anxious. 'At school?' she queried.

'No. Not at school.' Robert went down on his haunches beside her, putting himself on eye level terms with her.

'Miss Lawson is going to live with you and Mummy at Thorpe Hulme.'

Emma looked across at her mother for confirmation and Julie's heart went out to her. 'But – but Mummy said that when we came to England I would be able to go to a proper school!' she protested.

'Well, Mummy was wrong,' replied Robert abruptly, getting to his feet again.

'But why?' Emma was not to be put off. She tugged at his waistcoat. 'Come here again, Uncle Robert.' She pointed down to the floor beside her and goodnaturedly Robert resumed his earlier position.

'What now?'

Emma put her hands on his shoulders, experimentally poking her fingers in his ears. 'Why can't I go to school as well?'

Robert sighed and Lucy clicked her tongue, lifting the lid of the teapot and examining the contents. 'Stop asking silly questions, Emma. Uncle Robert knows best.'

Robert put his hands on Emma's small waist and when he straightened this time she was in his arms, her arms round his neck with a curious kind of possession. Watching them together, Julie wondered whether Emma found in Robert a counterpart of Michael. Or was it something more than that? Certainly Robert had plenty of patience with her and the child responded to that.

'Put her down, Robert. She's not a baby!' exclaimed Lucy irritably, but Robert ignored her, talking to Emma, making her giggle and hide her face in his neck.

Julie couldn't go on watching them. It was too painful an experience. 'If you'll excuse me,' she began, when Lucy said:

'Have you and Sandra been getting to know one another?'

Julie sighed. 'A little,' she admitted.

'Sandra's an old friend of Pamela's,' Lucy went on, conversationally. 'They used to go to school together. But Sandra chose to make child care her career instead of marriage.' She smiled benignly. 'I'm sure you'll find she's very efficient.'

'I'm sure I shall.' Julie clenched her fists. She might have known from the young woman's attitude that there was more to her dislike than mere antipathy. No doubt she was being placed in the household as a permanent watchdog, a kind of gaoler! Julie wanted to scream. What did they think she was? What did they expect her to do?

Taking a breath, she looked towards Emma, still in Robert's arms. 'Come along, darling,' she said. 'You need a wash before tea.'

Emma clung to Robert in the way children do when confronted by something they don't particularly care for, but to Julie it was the last straw. Gathering her gloves and handbag, she went out of the room and closed the doors firmly behind her before her emotions caused her to make an even bigger fool of herself than she had already done.

Whether or not Robert told his mother who Julie had been lunching with Lucy said nothing about the affair to her. Julie decided she could not have been told. She would never have allowed that to go unchallenged. Her heart lifted a little until she realized that Robert's motives for remaining silent were no doubt to prevent a rift between his mother and Pamela's father.

Later that evening, Julie dined with her mother-in-law. Robert had left to take Sandra Lawson home and was apparently going straight on to Orpington to see Pamela. Emma was in bed. Julie was rather concerned about her. She had eaten very little tea, and had complained of a headache. Julie thought the long day out had been too much for her, but she could hardly comment on that to Lucy.

They were in the lounge, watching television, when Emma started to cough, then choke, and cry out loudly. Julie leapt out of her chair, wrenched open the lounge doors and sped to Emma's room followed closely by her mother-in-law. But when she opened the door of the child's room the sight that met her eyes caused her to halt and utter a helpless exclamation. Emma had been sick, violently sick, and her bed was in wild disorder. She herself was pale and tearful, her fingers pressed to her trembling mouth in silent consternation at what she had done.

'Oh, Emma!' Julie shook her head sympathetically, but Lucy was horrified.

'You naughty girl!' she exclaimed, wrinkling her nose in distaste. 'Oh, you naughty little girl! Why didn't you go to the bathroom?'

Emma burst into more tears and Julie swung round on her mother-in-law fiercely. 'Is that all you can say?' she demanded angrily. 'Can't you see how upset and frightened she is? You know how children hate being sick!'

Lucy put a hand to her throat. 'That's not the point! If she had known she was going to be sick, she should have gone to the bathroom. Look at the carpet! The bedcovers! Everything's ruined!'

'Don't be so ridiculous!' snapped Julie. 'They'll clean. Besides, it's all your fault. You've been plying her with ice cream and fizzy drinks and sweets all day!'

'I didn't know this would happen!' retorted Lucy, regarding the child with something like dislike. 'If she'd been brought up to have a little self-control—'

'What's going on here?'

The brusque masculine tones were like a douche of cold water on the two women and Julie turned defensively, prepared to fight Robert too if necessary. But Robert merely propelled her aside and looked into Emma's bedroom himself.

'Oh, Emma!' he exclaimed, shaking his head, and advancing towards her. 'What on earth has been going on here? Someone's been sick all over your bed.' His voice was gentle as he looked round the room and his eyes alighted on a teddy bear she had been playing with earlier. 'Who was it? Teddy? Or was it that naughty doll sitting on the chair?'

Emma scrambled off the bed and made for him, uncaring of the fact that she was wet and sticky, flinging herself against his legs and hugging him tightly. 'It – it was Teddy,' she said, taking panting breaths. 'He – he had too many sweeties today.'

'Did he?' Robert smoothed his hands over the straight black tangled hair, and Julie supported herself weakly against the door jamb.

'Robert, for heaven's sake, stop comforting the child!' exclaimed his mother. 'Can't you see – she's wetting your trousers!'

Robert looked round, his hands still caressing Emma's head and shoulders, soothing her. Ignoring his mother's outburst, he said: 'Go and tell Halbird I want to see him. Tell him to bring some buckets of hot water and disinfectant, and some clean cloths.'

Lucy hesitated, and then as Robert's expression hardened, she muttered something uncomplimentary to herself and went away. Julie continued to lean against the door jamb, shaken after her skirmish with Lucy.

Robert prised Emma's fingers from his legs and looked down at her, a whimsical smile touching his lips. 'Come on!' he said. 'Let's go and clean you up.'

Emma gave her mother an appealing glance and Julie followed them into the softly tinted lights of the bathroom. Robert ran warm water into the step-in bath, adding a generous amount of bath salts so that the air was filled with scented steam, and then he took off Emma's pyjamas and put her into the soapy suds.

With her hair wet and secured on top of her head with an elastic band Robert found in his pocket, her pale cheeks looking a little less waxen, Emma was adorable, and Julie watched them with an aching pain in the pit of her stomach. Robert was kneeling at the side of the bath. He had shed his sheepskin coat, and seemed to care little that his navy corded trousers were wet now as well as everything else.

Halbird came to the door of the bathroom. He winked at Emma and said: 'Shall I start clearing up, sir?'

Robert looked up and grinned. It was the first time Julie had seen such a relaxed expression on his face and it was disturbingly attractive. 'If you would, Halbird,' he answered. 'I'll give you a hand myself when I've finished here.'

Julie glanced down at her long black skirt and white blouse. Pushing back the long sleeves of the blouse, she said: 'I'll help you, Halbird.'

'No.' Robert got to his feet. 'No, I'll help him.' He looked down at Emma. 'Mummy will get you out of there and dry you,' he said. 'I'll come and see you when you're into bed, right?'

'She can sleep with me,' said Julie, but again Robert shook his head.

'She can have my bed,' he said, drying his hands on a fluffy orange towel. 'Just for tonight while her room is dried and aired. I can sleep on the couch in the lounge.'

Halbird had disappeared to begin cleaning up and Julie made a helpless gesture. 'You can't do that, Robert. It's not necessary.'

Robert's eyes darkened. 'What do you suggest? Shall I share your bed? Don't press me too hard, Julie, or I might do just that, and that would do neither of us any good, would it?'

CHAPTER SEVEN

JULIE moved into the house at Thorpe Hulme at the weekend.

Her furniture had been delivered, so Lucy advised her, a couple of days earlier, and a housekeeper by the name of Mrs. Hudson was already in residence. As Julie had not wanted a housekeeper any more than she wanted a governess for Emma it aroused a fleeting sense of frustration inside her, but later, as she reviewed the situation, she decided that a housekeeper might come in useful. After all, if she was to get a job and support herself, she could hardly run the house as well.

Since the night Emma had been ill, she had scarcely seen Robert at all. Lucy had told her irritably that Robert had slept on the couch in the lounge that night, and it was obvious that she disapproved.

Robert himself did not refer to it. He was away most days at the office anyway, and his evenings seemed taken up with Pamela and her friends. Which was only natural, Julie told herself bitterly.

In actual fact, it was rather nice moving into her own home again. And Mrs. Hudson turned out to be not at all the sort of person she had expected after meeting Sandra Lawson. The housekeeper was a middle-aged widow, whose family were all grown up and married, and she treated Julie from the beginning more like a daughter than an employer.

It was arranged that Robert should drive them down to Thorpe Hulme on the Sunday morning, but on Friday evening he received a telegram from his New York office advising him of a meeting which he wanted to attend. Pamela, who was at the apartment when the telegram arrived, waiting for Robert to take her to the theatre, immediately essayed that he must go and that she would drive Julie and Emma down to the house herself.

'After all, darling,' she went on, 'it doesn't really matter who takes Julie down, does it?'

Robert did not reply for a moment, and then he shrugged. 'No, I suppose not,' he agreed. 'Is that all right with you, Julie?'

Julie wasn't particularly keen on having Pamela as her chauffeur. 'We could take a taxi,' she suggested.

Pamela spread her hands. 'My dear, that's not necessary. I'm free—' she glanced insinuatively at Robert – 'in more ways than one.'

Julie had perforce to accept her offer and so it was Pamela who drove her to the house and helped her carry her luggage inside.

Mrs. Hudson came to greet them from the direction of the kitchen. She was small, like Julie, but much more rotund, with greying hair and a warm and smiling countenance. She gave Emma a particularly welcoming smile and then said:

'I've made some coffee, Mrs. Pemberton. It's waiting for you in the lounge. Would the little one like to come to the kitchen with me? I've been baking and there's a nice jammy doughnut if she'd like one.'

Emma's eyes widened. 'Oh, super!' she exclaimed, and Julie said:

'Well, all right. But don't overdo it, will you?'

'I'll see she doesn't,' promised Mrs. Hudson, and somehow Julie knew she would. She was exactly the sort of person she would have chosen as Emma's grandmother, and she felt a twinge of guilt at this realization.

After they had gone, Julie looked round the hall with some pleasure. Here the walls were all white, while a dark red carpet flowed into every corner and up the attractive staircase.

Pamela led the way into the lounge. The carpet and furnishings she had chosen looked warm and welcoming, and Pamela made herself very much at home at once, seating herself on the couch beside the coffee tray, almost as though she was welcoming Julie into her house.

But Julie refused to feel exasperated. It didn't matter what any of them said or did now. She and Emma had a home of their own and for part of the day at least they would not have to consider anybody but themselves.

After she had handed Julie her coffee and Julie had seated herself in an armchair by the windows, Pamela said: 'I think you're going to be very comfortable here, aren't you?'

Julie managed a faint smile. 'I think so. It's a lovely old house.'

'Yes, it is. I wanted Robert to buy it for us at first, but he said it would be too small.'

Julie sipped her coffee. 'I see.'

'Well, after all, Robert has to do a certain amount of entertaining, and at the moment he's confined to his apartment. Once we're married I expect we shall be able to entertain more fully – have people to stay, and so on. A bachelor doesn't think about these things, does he?'

Julie shook her head politely.

Pamela studied her for a long moment, making Julie feel rather uncomfortable, and then she said: 'You were once engaged to Robert, weren't you?'

Julie put down her coffee cup with rather a clatter in her saucer. 'Yes, that's right.'

Pamela looked thoughtful. 'I know. Robert told me.'

Julie swallowed with difficulty. The idea of Robert discussing her with his fiancée was not an acceptable one. She wondered why Pamela was bringing this up.

'But you married his brother,' she went on.

'Michael. Yes,' Julie nodded.

'Robert said you split up before he went overseas on an assignment for the company. To Venezuela.'

'Yes, we did.'

'Do you mind telling me why?' Pamela's eyes were calculating.

Julie made a helpless movement of her shoulders. 'Does it matter?'

Pamela's lips tightened. 'I'd like to know.'

'Why don't you ask Robert?'

'I have. He said—' she hesitated – 'he said you called the whole thing off.'

Julie's cheeks burned. 'I see.'

'Is that the truth?'

'Well – yes.'

'Then why?' Pamela frowned.

Julie sighed. She didn't know how to answer her. On impulse, she said: 'Surely it's obvious, isn't it? I – I had fallen in love with Michael.'

Pamela's face cleared. 'Oh, I'm sorry,' she exclaimed, obviously relieved. 'Of course. I'm afraid I never thought of that. I should have done, shouldn't I? Because you married Michael before Robert returned from his assignment, didn't you?'

Julie nodded, finding it hard to articulate. 'Well, Robert was away six months,' she replied tightly.

'Yes, so he said. I suppose in other circumstances you'd have gone with him, wouldn't you?'

Julie wished she'd change the subject. 'Do you have a cigarette?' she asked, linking and unlinking her fingers.

Pamela frowned, but she felt about in her handbag and brought out a packet. Once they were both smoking, she said: 'You didn't mind my asking, did you? Only – well, it's difficult to discuss this sort of thing with Robert.'

Julie exhaled smoke into the atmosphere jerkily. 'No,

that's all right,' she said, getting restlessly to her feet. 'Do you – do you think we're going to have a hard winter? I can't remember what it's like to have snow.'

Pamela rose too, joining her at the window. 'I've never said anything,' she said gently, 'but I'm offering my condolences now, on the death of your husband. I – I'm sorry I never had the chance to meet him.'

Julie stared at her blankly. What did one say to that? 'Thank you,' she murmured awkwardly.

Pamela nodded and touched her shoulder in almost a friendly fashion. 'And now I must go. Mummy is expecting me back for drinks before lunch. We've got some people coming in.' She hesitated. 'Once you've settled down here, you must come over and see us. I'm sure Mummy and Daddy would be delighted to welcome you.'

What a *volte-face*! Julie was astounded. It was obvious so long as one did not get in Pamela's way she could be as charming as her father.

And thinking of Francis, Julie realized this was her opportunity to mention that she had had lunch with him earlier in the week. But somehow the words would not come. And after all, Francis himself had not mentioned it obviously, so how could she?

Pamela moved to the door and calling good-bye to Emma and the housekeeper she left. Julie watched her drive away with some misgivings. What a terrible complicated life it suddenly seemed! What was wrong with her that she should find she preferred Pamela's hostility to her friendship?

During the next few days, they settled in at Thorpe Hulme. Sandra Lawson was not joining them until they had had a week to adjust themselves, so for those first few days there was just Julie, Emma and Mrs. Hudson.

The gardens at the back of the house enchanted Emma. Although the days were cold and chilly, the swing proved an irresistible magnet and she spent part of every day on it, usually accompanied by either Mrs. Hudson or her mother.

There were orchards, too, of apple and pear trees, and a sun house which would be ideal as a playroom for Emma in summer. Trellises of climbing roses divided the garden into separate areas and Mrs. Hudson suggested that they might ask the gardener, whom Robert had employed for her from the village, to grow some vegetables there the following year. Julie agreed, although there was a decidedly hollow feeling inside her when she contemplated the following year. Robert would be married by then, and whenever he came to see them no doubt Pamela would come, too. How would she ever be able to stand it?

Robert was still away in the United States. His visit had been prolonged to take in a trip to San Francisco, and it would be another week before he returned. Naturally, Julie did not hear from him direct, but Lucy rang almost every day to make sure Julie was kept up to date with news.

Pamela called a couple of times, too. Ostensibly her visits were to see how Julie was coping, but privately Julie thought she was inordinately curious about her sister-in-law-to-be, and she wanted to reassure herself that she had nothing to fear from that quarter. She made a point of discussing her and Robert's plans whenever she and Julie were alone together, and had she not been so friendly Julie would have suspected she was being deliberately unkind, gloating over her own happiness at a time when Julie would be feeling almost bereft.

But Julie kept these thoughts to herself and listened to what she had to say with outward detachment.

On Thursday, Francis rang her.

Answering the telephone disinterestedly, expecting to hear her mother-in-law's voice, Julie was pleasantly surprised to recognize his.

'Hello, Julie,' he said, and she could imagine the wry smile he would be wearing. 'Did you think I'd forgotten all about you?'

Julie moved her shoulders helplessly. 'No. I thought you'd had second thoughts,' she replied teasingly.

Francis laughed. 'Hardly. Well? How are you settling down to life in the country?'

'I like it.' Julie perched on the arm of an easy chair. 'We're settling down quite well. Emma adores the freedom.'

'I expect she does. I don't suppose she had much in Malaya.'

'Not really. She was always in the company of an *ayah*.' Julie tucked a strand of hair behind her ear. 'How are you?'

'Oh, struggling along,' he replied mockingly. 'The main reason I haven't rung is because I've been away, in Scotland. I only got back last night.'

'Robert's away, too.'

'Yes, I know. I hear of nothing else in our home.'

'Oh, sorry, of course!' Julie laughed herself now. 'I forgot about Pamela.'

'Did you really?' Francis was amused. 'No easy task, I do assure you.'

Julie laughed again. 'I'm glad you rang,' she said impulsively.

'Are you? Why?'

Julie sighed. 'Oh, I don't know. Just feeling a bit down, that's all. I guess it's the anticlimax of moving in. Oh – and of knowing the governess arrives on Sunday?'

'The governess? You mean – Sandra Lawson?'

'Yes. Do you know her?'

'Lord, yes. She and Pam went to school together.'

'That's right.' Julie recalled what her mother-in-law had said. 'I'd forgotten.'

'What's wrong? Does she intimidate you?'

Julie traced the pattern of the carpet with her toe. 'She's not going to,' she said determinedly.

'That sounds ominous.' Francis chuckled. 'Look, love, I didn't ring to spend half an hour chatting to you on the phone. I want to see you. When?'

Julie hesitated. 'I don't know. There's Emma—'

'Bring Emma, too. I tell you what – how about me coming down and you inviting me to lunch?'

Julie drew her brows together. 'I suppose you could,' she said slowly, mentally anticipating what Robert's reaction might be when he discovered from Emma, no doubt, that Francis had come for a meal.

'Don't sound too encouraging,' remarked Francis dryly. 'I might get the wrong impression.'

'Oh, Francis, I'm sorry.' Julie was laughingly apologetic. 'Of course you can come for lunch. And as a special treat I'll make you my *pièce de résistance*!'

'That sounds interesting. What is it?'

'Wait and see,' replied Julie. She glanced at her watch. 'It's eleven already. Where are you?'

'At home,' he answered nonchalantly.

'At home?' Julie was shocked.

'It's all right, I'm in my study. No one can hear us.'

'You make it sound so – so furtive.'

'Do I? I'm sorry. All right, I'll go out now and tell Louise and Pamela where I'm going, and no doubt they'll come with me.'

'Oh, Francis!'

'Do you want them to come?'

Julie sighed. 'Of course not.' She wanted to see Francis again, but Francis alone. He was so good for her, and she needed someone to talk to.

'Well, then?'

'Just come,' she said huskily, and rang off.

109

She had hardly time to change into a short-skirted red jersey dress and comb her hair before his car drew to a halt in front of the main door and Emma bounced through from the kitchen.

'Is this Uncle Francis?' she asked. Julie had had to tell Mrs. Hudson there was to be a guest for lunch, and Emma was obviously excited.

'That's right, darling,' she answered, and opened the door.

Francis looked years younger in cream casual trousers and a roll-collared brown jersey than in his formal town clothes, and Julie looked at him warmly.

'Hi, honey,' he said, tickling Emma under her chin and making her giggle. Then in an aside to Julie, he went on: 'Don't look at me like that, Julie, or I'll begin to wish I wasn't the nice guy you think I am.'

Julie smiled. 'Come along in,' she said, not at all disturbed by his easy familiarity. Somehow Francis was different from any other man she had ever known. 'I suppose you know your way around.'

Emma bounded ahead of them into the lounge and he surveyed the room critically. 'Yes, I know the place,' he agreed. 'This isn't bad, is it? Considering my daughter chose the decorations!'

Julie laughed and went across to the tray of drinks on the table in the corner. 'What can I offer you? Sherry? Scotch? Or would you prefer coffee?'

'Scotch will be fine. Can I sit down?'

'Of course.' Julie nodded and Francis subsided on to the couch with Emma beside him.

'Where's Auntie Pamela?' she asked, with her usual lack of tact.

Francis smiled. 'At home,' he replied complacently.

'Didn't she want to come with you?' Emma was surprised.

'Most likely, but I didn't ask her.' Francis accepted his Scotch from Julie, smiling more widely at her rueful expression. 'I thought – she's been to see Emma lots of times without asking me. Why should I ask her?'

Emma looked suitably gratified at this. 'Did you really come to see me?'

'And Mummy,' remarked Francis, sipping his Scotch. 'After all, it would be rude of me to say that I just came to see you, wouldn't it?' He winked at her. 'But we know, don't we?'

Emma gurgled with laughter and Julie sat down beside them. 'Why didn't you have more children, Francis?' she exclaimed, before she could stop herself and realize what an impertinent and personal question she was asking.

But Francis didn't seem to mind. 'It was not to be,' he remarked lightly, and Julie quickly changed the subject.

Lunch was a gay meal. Francis was adept at entertaining a child, and Emma obviously found him good company. After the dessert, a delicious strawberry shortcake which was Julie's *pièce de résistance*, she insisted on taking him outside and showing him her swing and when Julie looked out of the kitchen window she saw them chasing one another round the summer house.

Mrs. Hudson, who had not met Francis before today, gave Julie a strange look, and then said: 'He's a nice man, isn't he? Lots of patience.'

Julie sighed. 'Yes. You know he's Miss Hillingdon's father, don't you?'

Mrs. Hudson nodded. 'I realized that.'

'And I suppose you also realize that he shouldn't be here,' murmured Julie dryly.

'Why?' Mrs. Hudson was always direct.

Julie bent her head. 'Well – surely it's obvious. He has a wife, too, you know.'

Mrs. Hudson busied herself with the dishes. 'But it's not

like that between you two, is it?' she said.

Julie stared at her. 'How can you say that? You don't know the situation.'

Mrs. Hudson shook her head. 'I know enough about a man and a woman to know when they're sleeping together,' she replied firmly, and at Julie's startled gasp, she went on: 'Will Mr. Hillingdon be staying for dinner?'

Julie swallowed with difficulty. 'I – er – no, I shouldn't think so.'

Mrs. Hudson smiled. 'Don't look so shocked. I suppose I shouldn't have said anything, should I?'

Julie shrugged. 'I'm glad – at least, there's no one else I can talk to.'

Mrs. Hudson smiled more widely. 'Well, don't worry about me. I know when to keep my mouth shut.'

Julie gave her an exasperated look. 'That sounds terrible, do you know that?' Then she laughed. 'Oh, Mrs. Hudson, you're right. He is a nice man.'

When Francis and Emma returned to the house, Mrs. Hudson was preparing afternoon tea, and Francis sank wearily into a comfortable chair in the lounge.

'You've exhausted me!' he complained to Emma, who immediately switched on the television and took up a position that could not possibly be good for her eyes.

'It's almost time for Play School,' she explained, smiling at him. 'You're not really tired, are you, Uncle Francis?'

'You've got to be joking!' Francis regarded her in horror. 'I'm not used to spending the afternoon dashing round the garden.'

'It will do you good,' said Emma practically, repeating the words that had from time to time been said to her.

'I'm glad you think so.' Francis looked up at Julie who had come in with the tea trolley. 'Is there a cup for me?'

'Of course.' Julie smiled. 'Are you going to stay for dinner?'

Francis lost his bantering expression. 'I'd like nothing more,' he answered honestly, 'but I have to take Louise out this evening. We usually play bridge on Thursdays.'

Julie nodded, not altogether disappointed. 'Never mind.'

Francis glanced at Emma, saw she was engrossed in her television programme, and reaching over took Julie's hand. 'Oh, Julie!' he exclaimed impatiently. 'Ask me to stay, and I'll stay.'

Julie withdrew her hand reluctantly. 'Do you take sugar?' she asked, breathing a little quickly herself.

Francis nodded. 'Two, please.' He sighed. 'Let me take you out to dinner. One evening this week. Before the dragon arrives.' She knew he was referring to Sandra Lawson, and her lips twitched momentarily. 'How about Saturday? That's a good evening. Wouldn't you like to get dressed up and go on the town? I'm sure Mrs. Hudson could cope with Emma.'

'I'm sure she could.' Julie ran her tongue over her dry lips. 'It sounds – marvellous.'

'It will be,' he promised.

'All right, then. I'll ask her before you leave.'

'Good.' Francis took his cup of tea. 'Believe me, the days will drag until then.'

After Francis had gone, after the arrangements had been made with Mrs. Hudson, Julie felt terribly guilty. Once she had settled Emma down for the night, instead of going into the lounge as she usually did, she went into the kitchen. Mrs. Hudson was washing up the dinner dishes, and looked up with a smile.

'Is there something you want, Mrs. Pemberton?' she asked.

'Just a chat,' answered Julie, sighing and taking up a tea towel and beginning to dry the dishes on the draining board.

'That's not necessary, you know,' exclaimed the housekeeper. 'Talk if you want to, but I'll manage these.'

'I'd like to help,' said Julie simply, and Mrs. Hudson said no more. 'I – I was sick of my own company.'

'Emma settled down all right?'

'Oh, yes. She was worn out. It's been a pretty strenuous day for her.'

'And for Mr. Hillingdon, too, I shouldn't wonder,' observed Mrs. Hudson with a short laugh. 'Fair wore him out, she did.'

Julie smiled. 'He is good with her, isn't he?'

'Yes, ma'am. He should have had some youngsters of his own.'

'Well, he had Pamela, years ago.'

'Yes.' Mrs. Hudson's tone was revealing.

'Don't you like her?' Julie was committing the unforgivable sin of gossiping about her guests with her servant, but she couldn't prevent the question.

Mrs. Hudson pulled a wry face. 'Well, let's say she's not my cup of tea,' she answered diplomatically.

Julie nodded. 'I know what you mean. A sort of – *I do not like thee, Dr. Fell* – kind of personality.'

'That's right.' The housekeeper squeezed out her dishcloth and began to mop the draining board. 'But no doubt I'm wrong. Mr. Robert seems to like her well enough.'

'You know – Robert?'

'Bless you, yes. I used to work for his mother, years ago. When both he and Michael were toddlers.'

'Did you really?' Julie was fascinated. 'Oh, go on! Tell me about it.'

'About Michael, ma'am?'

Julie coloured. 'Both of them.'

Mrs. Hudson shrugged. 'Well, they were little rips, that I do remember. Just a year between them, you know, and ripe for mischief.'

'You can't have been very old yourself then.'

'No, I wasn't. Seventeen or eighteen, that's all. I was in service with Mrs. Pemberton senior.'

'I see.' Julie made a helpless gesture. 'Heavens, what a small world it really is.'

Mrs. Hudson nodded. 'Well, when Mr. Robert bought this house and was looking for a housekeeper, he came straight to me.'

Julie perched on a high kitchen stool. 'Did you see much of them in later years?'

'From time to time they'd come to see us, after I was married, you know. And when my Brian died, they were very kind.' The housekeeper gave a reminiscent smile. 'They always were nice boys.'

'Yes.' Julie tipped her head on one side. 'Did you know I was once engaged to Robert?'

Mrs. Hudson finished emptying her water and began to dry her hands. 'Yes, I knew that, ma'am. I even received an invitation to the wedding.'

Julie's cheeks flushed. 'Oh!'

Mrs. Hudson sighed. 'I would never have dreamed it would all be called off like that, and Mr. Robert going to Venezuela and all.'

Julie slid off the stool. 'It was his decision.'

'What? To go to Venezuela?'

'Yes. And to call off the wedding.'

'But I understood he had to go, ma'am. There was an accident, wasn't there? One of his men was killed, wasn't he?'

'Yes. On the Guaba river valley project.'

'That's right.' Mrs. Hudson warmed to her subject. 'And Mr. Robert had to go out and take his place.'

'He didn't *have* to,' stated Julie stoically.

Mrs. Hudson looked perturbed. 'Oh, I don't know about that, ma'am. After all, sending out someone else would have been risky, wouldn't it? Particularly as he himself was the only person to know all about the job. Apart from the man who was killed, of course.'

Julie shrugged. 'Well, it was all a long time ago.'

Mrs. Hudson nodded. 'Yes, and you couldn't have loved him, could you, ma'am, 'cos you married Mr. Michael and went off with him before Mr. Robert got back.'

Julie moved towards the door. 'Robert went away exactly one week before our wedding,' she said through stiff lips. 'Would your husband have done that?'

Mrs. Hudson frowned. 'That's a difficult question to answer, ma'am. You mean – you and he quarrelled, because of this trip?'

Julie caught her breath. 'I didn't say that.' Mrs. Hudson was too perceptive.

Mrs. Hudson shrugged. 'Well, you know your own business best, ma'am. Like I said, you couldn't have married Mr. Michael like you did, unless you'd had some doubts about Mr. Robert.'

Julie opened the door. 'No, well, let's not discuss it any further, shall we? You can finish now, if you like. If I want anything later, I'll get it myself.'

'All right, Mrs. Pemberton, thank you.' Mrs. Hudson took off her apron and folded it into a drawer. 'I shall probably pop down to Mrs. Fielding in the village for an hour.'

'That's fine.' Julie allowed the door to swing closed behind her and made her way back to the lounge. But suddenly the idea of spending a lonely vigil watching television had lost its appeal, and by nine o'clock she was climbing between the sheets, dry-eyed but depressed.

Sandra Lawson arrived without warning on Saturday morning.

Mrs. Hudson admitted her and Julie encountered her in the hall. 'I hope you don't object, Mrs. Pemberton,' she said, standing down her suitcases. 'But my landlady wanted to re-let my flat from today, so I thought, rather than waste money spending the night at a hotel, I'd come here. After all, one day more or less won't make any difference, will it?'

Julie made a confused gesture. 'I – well – Mrs. Hudson?'

The housekeeper shrugged her ample shoulders. 'The bed's all made up, ma'am. No problem there.'

Sandra gave Mrs. Hudson an appraising stare. 'You must be Mrs. Hudson. Miss Hillingdon told me about you.'

Mrs. Hudson inclined her head in assent. 'That's right, miss.'

Julie twisted her fingers together. 'Well, I don't suppose it matters,' she said at last. 'Mrs. Hudson, would you show Miss Lawson her room and then make us some coffee?'

'Very good, Mrs. Pemberton.'

Mrs. Hudson indicated that Sandra should follow her up the stairs, but she made no attempt to assist her with her cases. Julie hesitated, uncertain of her own position, and then shrugging, walked back into the lounge as Sandra hoisted her own cases and followed the housekeeper with ill-grace. It was not an auspicious beginning.

Julie stood in the lounge, staring unseeingly out of the window. Sandra's arrival was going to create difficulties. Tonight, for instance, she was supposed to be going out with Francis. How could she do that without Sandra being aware of her escort, and he was Pamela's father, after all. But there were other, more personal problems.

Now that Sandra was here could she go off and leave her alone on her first evening? And if she did, what of her arrangement with Mrs. Hudson regarding Emma? Sandra might decide she was more suited to putting the child to bed in Julie's absence than the housekeeper, and somehow Julie didn't think Emma would care for that. They hadn't discussed the governess's arrival in any detail, but she had sensed that Emma had not exactly taken to Sandra Lawson.

It was all very upsetting and annoying and Julie wished there was someone she could confide in.

Emma came into the room, flushed and grubby from the garden. 'Who was that in the taxi, Mummy?' she asked, frowning.

Julie sighed. 'It was Miss Lawson, darling.'

'But I thought you said she was coming tomorrow.'

'I did. And she was. But the arrangements have been changed.'

Emma grimaced. 'Why? Will I have to do lessons today?'

'Don't be silly, darling. I don't suppose you'll start lessons for a few days yet. And look at those shoes of yours! They're filthy! Go and put your slippers on if you're staying indoors.'

'Oh, all right.'

Emma trudged moodily out of the room and Julie watched her go with an indulgent expression. Poor Emma! So many things had changed in such a short period of time. First Rhatoon, then Kuala Lumpur, London, and finally Thorpe Hulme. Was she beginning to doubt that anything would ever settle down to a routine again?

On impulse, she dialled Robert's London apartment. Halbird answered and Julie said: 'Is Mrs. Pemberton there?'

'Sorry, ma'am, no. She's out this morning. Shall I tell her you want to speak to her when she comes back?'

Julie hesitated. 'Er – no – no, that won't be necessary, Halbird. Thanks.'

'Very good, ma'am. It's nice to hear from you again. Are you settled down now?'

'More or less,' answered Julie wryly. ' 'Bye.'

After she had replaced the receiver she stared at it for

several minutes, biting her lip. Obviously Robert had not yet returned from the States or Halbird would have mentioned it. She picked up the telephone directory and searching found the Hillingdons' number. She stared at it for a long moment. Dared she telephone Francis? What if Pamela answered, or Louise? What excuse could she give for phoning?

Then she thought of his office. He might be there, and if not they could perhaps tell her where she might get in touch with him direct.

The receptionist at the Hillingdon corporation building was very correct. 'Mr. Hillingdon is in the building, miss,' she said. 'But he's not taking any calls. He's in conference. Can I take a message?'

Julie sighed. 'Wouldn't it be possible for you to tell him I'm calling and ask him when it's convenient to speak to him?'

The receptionist hesitated. Obviously she was uncertain as to Julie's identity, even though she had given her name, and to the importance attached to it. 'Just a minute, miss,' she said, and cut Julie off from the exchange.

Julie waited impatiently and while she did so Emma came back in, her hands and face clean now, and warm slippers on her feet. 'Who're you ringing?' she whispered.

'Never mind,' mouthed Julie.

'Is it Grandma?'

'No. Be quiet.' Julie heaved another sigh. How much longer was she going to have to wait?

It could only have been seconds before she had her reply. Francis's calm voice came over the wire. 'Julie? Is that you?'

'Francis!' Julie was so relieved she sank down on to the arm of a chair nearby. 'Heavens, it's like trying to speak to royalty, getting through to you!'

Francis chuckled. 'Well, I was in conference,' he said gently.

'I know. I'm sorry I disturbed you.'

'Don't be silly.' Francis was reassuringly unperturbed. 'What's wrong?'

Julie glanced helplessly at Emma and then said: 'Well, it's difficult to talk right now. But actually, Miss Lawson has arrived today.'

Francis sounded unconcerned. 'So what?'

'Well, surely it's obvious.'

'You mean about tonight, of course.'

'Yes.' Julie sighed. 'Oh, Francis, what am I going to do?'

'You're going to have dinner with me, of course, what else?' His tone was firm now.

'But how can I? She'll know who you are.'

'So what?'

'Francis, please!'

'Look, Julie, I explained to you before – I don't care who knows about our association. It's you I care about.' He sighed now. 'Look, if what you mean is you'd rather call it off because of this woman – well, that's a different matter.'

'Oh, Francis!' Julie gripped the phone tightly.

'Look, if it makes you any happier I'll suggest to Pamela that she drives over there this afternoon. When she sees Sandra, she's sure to invite her back, particularly as Robert's away. How would that be?'

'Oh, that's marvellous!' Julie breathed more easily, and then became aware that Sandra Lawson had entered the room as she was speaking. 'Look, I – er – I've got to go now.'

'I understand you.' Francis laughed. 'Oh, what a tangled web, indeed.'

Julie laughed softly, and rang off. Then she turned to the other girl. 'Everything all right?'

Sandra seated herself uninvited on the couch. 'Fine,

thanks.' She looked at Emma. 'Hello, Emma! We must get to know one another.'

'Yes.' Emma was doubtful. 'Are you going to live here?'

'That's right.' Sandra seemed quite at home. 'And later on you can show me where we're going to do our lessons. Has Mummy set a room aside for them?'

Julie cleared her throat. 'Well, actually, not all the rooms are furnished,' she said. 'I – er – Mr. Pemberton thought I would prefer to choose some of my own furnishings. This room and the dining room are furnished downstairs, but upstairs only three of the bedrooms have been furnished. I'm afraid for the time being you'll have to make do with this room, or the dining room.'

Sandra frowned. 'Then it will have to be the dining room. We can't possibly work where there are no tables. Emma will need a firm surface to work on.'

'Well, I hope to get up to town within the next week or so and choose some fittings,' said Julie quickly. 'Perhaps it will not be too much of a hardship, and besides, Emma needs time to get used to the idea. Maybe you could concentrate on more practical things until I've had time to organize myself.'

'But you've been here a week, haven't you?' the other girl queried insolently.

'Yes.' Julie looked up with relief to see Mrs. Hudson entering the room with a tray of coffee. 'Oh, good. Put it down here, Mrs. Hudson.'

'Very good, ma'am.' Mrs. Hudson looked at Emma. 'Do you want to come and help me make some pastry?'

'Ooh, yes, can I?' Emma sprang to her feet, but Sandra Lawson halted her.

'Emma and I are just getting to know one another, Mrs. Hudson,' she said sharply.

Julie looked at them all rather wryly. 'I think Emma's

going to have plenty of time to get to know you, Sandra,' she said. 'Go along, darling.'

Emma skipped out of the room after the housekeeper and Sandra gave Julie an intimidating stare. 'How am I expected to have any control over the child if you're going to countermand my instructions?' she asked sharply.

Julie shook her head, refusing to get angry. 'Allowing Emma to help Mrs. Hudson is not countermanding your instructions. You've only just got here, Sandra. Don't press Emma too hard yet.' She might have added: *Or me either*, but she didn't.

Their conversation after that was stilted. Obviously Sandra was still smarting from a sense of injustice and Julie was engrossed with her thoughts, looking ahead with depressing clarity to years of this woman's undiluted company. How would she ever stand it?

As Francis had promised, Pamela arrived that afternoon and expressed delight at seeing Sandra. Julie left them together, and sought Mrs. Hudson's company in the kitchen.

Emma was playing in the garden and Julie watched her silently for a few moments until Mrs. Hudson said: 'What about tonight, ma'am? Are you still going out?'

'Yes.' Julie turned to her. 'I – er – I spoke to Francis on the phone this morning. He suggested sending Pamela over here this afternoon. They're old friends, you know, Sandra Lawson and Pamela, and as Robert's away he thought she might possibly invite Sandra back there for a meal this evening.'

Mrs. Hudson chuckled. 'Devious!'

'Yes, it is rather. But I shouldn't have cared to leave Emma to her on her first night here, apart from the other considerations, of course.'

'Yes, ma'am.' Mrs. Hudson sighed. 'But if you don't like her, why have you got her here?'

122

'It was Robert's idea, apparently. I had no choice. He is Emma's legal guardian.'

'And no better one,' commented Mrs. Hudson dryly.

'What do you mean?' Julie turned to her, her cheeks flushing.

'Nothing, ma'am. Just that he's a suitable person to have charge of the child.'

'I'm her mother!'

'I know. But a child needs a man.'

Julie sighed. 'I see.' Her colour subsided again.

'What did you think I meant, Mrs. Pemberton?'

Julie shrugged. 'I don't know.' She walked to the door. 'I'll go and take a bath. If you want me, you know where I am.'

To Julie's relief, Pamela did suggest that Sandra might like to dine with them that evening, but she was disconcerted when Pamela went on: 'Why don't you come, too, Julie? Daddy's going out, so there'll just be the four of us women. We could have a cosy chat.'

Julie doubted whether any chat she could share with these women would be cosy, but she had to think carefully before replying.

'Actually — actually an old friend rang this morning,' she said, 'and suggested calling round this evening. So I don't think I'd better go out, do you?'

Pamela frowned. 'I suppose not.' She rubbed her palms together thoughtfully. 'An old friend, you say.'

'Someone I — I used to work with,' said Julie hastily.

'At Pembertons?' Pamela was annoyingly inquisitive.

'Yes.'

'Do I know her?'

'I don't suppose so.' Julie hated this. 'She — she left there some time ago. Er — Valerie Smith.'

'No, I don't know the name.' Pamela shook her head. 'Well, Sandra, we ought to be going.'

'Yes.' Sandra rose to her feet. 'You're sure you don't mind, Mrs. Pemberton?'

'Of course not.' Julie just wanted them to go. They were beginning to get on her nerves.

It was with relief she heard Pamela's car pull away and she went back into the lounge feeling rather limp. Emma climbed on to her knee as she sat down, and she hugged her lovingly.

'I wish that Miss Lawson wasn't going to stay with us,' she said gloomily. 'Don't you, Mummy?'

Julie sighed. 'She's only the governess, Emma. Nothing's going to be any different because of her.'

'I shall have to do lessons.'

'Yes, well, you would anyway, at school,' remarked Julie reasonably. 'But after the lessons are over, everything will be just the same. I promise.'

Emma was asleep before Julie began to get ready for her dinner date. She had mentioned nothing to her about going out, mainly to avoid questions, but Mrs. Hudson had instructions to tell her exactly where she was if she woke up and started to worry.

Julie dressed in a simple gown of cream wool, with long sleeves and a low round neckline, the long skirt of which emphasized the slender curve of her hips and the narrowness of her waist. She had put on a little weight since her arrival in England, and it suited her.

Francis arrived soon after seven and complimented her on her appearance. 'But then you always look good,' he remarked dryly, and Julie was pleased.

They dined in town, at quite a well known restaurant, and Julie looked perturbed when several people came to speak to him and looked at Julie with open curiosity.

'Don't look so worried!' he chided her gently. 'This is a good feeling you're giving me. I thought I was past the age for such things.'

'You're not old,' protested Julie, laughingly.

'I'm forty-eight, and you're what? Twenty-five, twenty-six?' She nodded. 'More than twenty years older than you are. Old enough to be your father, in fact.'

Julie put her hand across the table and touched his. 'Age is only relative,' she said. 'You don't look old, and you don't act old. Why should you assume you're any different from anyone else? From me? There are times when I feel positively senile.'

Francis grinned. 'Like I said, you're very good for me.'

Later, they danced. The music was slow and languid, and Julie felt relaxed in his arms. She realized she felt affection for him, and the knowledge was warming. She wasn't in love with him, but their relationship was something special, something good.

He drove her home around midnight, but she didn't invite him in for a drink. Somehow she sensed that whatever it was she felt for him could easily be confused with the real thing in this mellow, drowsy state she was in, and she wasn't at all sure that Francis would be able to resist touching her, particularly as part of her longed to be loved. If she encouraged him now, she would surely regret it later.

He drove away as she let herself into the house. There were lights in the lounge, and she guessed Mrs. Hudson was watching the late movie. She thrust open the door, and peeped inside, not wanting to startle her in case she was asleep, and then uttered a gasp of surprise. The lamplit room looked warm and comfortable, and as though to prove it, Robert was stretched out lazily on the couch, fast asleep.

CHAPTER EIGHT

JULIE stared down at his face, relaxed and vulnerable somehow in sleep, for a long time. It was obvious from the lines around his eyes that he had not slept much while he was away, and he looked exhausted.

As her gaze eventually moved round the room, she saw more evidence of his occupation. His jacket was slung carelessly over the back of an armchair while his shoes were kicked haphazardly on to the rug before the hearth. His cigar case and lighter lay on the low table beside the couch together with a dirty cup and a pot of coffee which bore witness to the fact that Mrs. Hudson had provided something for him before she retired. But what was he doing here? Why had he come? When had he arrived back from the States? Not this afternoon, surely, or Pamela would have known.

She looked down at him again, moving silently into the room to stand beside the couch. He had loosened his tie and folded back his shirt cuffs. His shirt was partially unfastened, too, revealing the brown, hair-covered skin of his chest. He looked absurdly young and she felt a compelling desire to touch him, to make him aware of her. But she also knew that once he saw her that cold, cynical expression would enter his eyes and she would feel unutterably devastated.

As though becoming aware of her concentrated scrutiny, his eyes suddenly opened, flickering lazily. Julie stiffened, standing completely still as his gaze steadied and moved up over her to her face.

'Julie!' he exclaimed, blinking, still half unaware of his surroundings. He propped himself up on one elbow, frowning in the effort to remember his whereabouts, and then groaned, 'God, my head!' and fell back against the cushions again.

Julie was concerned. Seating herself on the edge of the wide couch, she put her hand to his forehead and found it was burning hot. But Robert took her hand and moved it to his cheek, turning his lips into the palm so that she trembled in his grasp. His eyes were half-closed and drowsy, and she was sure he didn't know what he was doing.

'Robert,' she protested half-heartedly, trying to withdraw from him, but he reached out, sliding his hands possessively over her body, drawing her inexorably down to him. His hand behind her head propelled her mouth to his, and then he rolled over, imprisoning her beneath him, kissing her until she was weak and clinging to him.

'I want to love you,' he groaned thickly, burying his face in her hair. 'I can't help it. You're driving me crazy, do you know that?'

The weight of his body on hers was a potent seducement, and Julie wanted to submit. She wanted to let him do what he liked with her and to hell with the consequences. But the thought of Emma, and what the consequences had meant the last time she had let him drown her reason in passion, were sufficient to destroy the intimacy of the moment.

Taking advantage of his momentary weakness, she managed to get her feet to the floor and half slid, half flung herself off the couch. Robert remained where she had left him, watching her as she smoothed her dress over her hips and ran an unsteady hand over her hair. His expression now was daunting.

'What's wrong?' he demanded harshly. 'Am I too late this evening? Was Francis all you expected him to be?'

Julie gasped. Picking up a cushion, she flung it at him angrily, following it with a book. 'How dare you suggest such a thing?'

Robert warded off her missiles and rose to his feet, swaying for a moment as his head obviously pained him. 'What am I supposed to think?' he asked bleakly. Then: 'Why the hell did you go out with him again? What are you trying to do to me?'

'To you?' Julie's breasts rose and fell quickly beneath the soft material of her gown.

'Yes, to me.' Robert raked his hair back. 'God, Julie, don't you know that the thought of you with another man—' He broke off. 'Are you in love with him?'

Julie pressed the palms of her hands to her cheeks. 'Of course not.'

'No more than you were in love with Michael,' he muttered violently. 'God, Julie, it's just as well you and Michael were in Malaya when I got back from Venezuela or I'd have killed you both!' He pressed a hand to his head in agony. 'Oh, lord, have you got anything for a headache? My head feels as though it's splitting in two!'

Julie hesitated and then sped across the room to the door. She knew Mrs. Hudson had some aspirins in the kitchen. She had seen them on the shelf above the draining board.

When she arrived back with the bottle of aspirins and some water in a glass Robert was stretched out on the couch again. She put down the things on the table beside him and looked down at him doubtfully. 'How long is it since you had any sleep?' she asked. 'Real sleep, I mean. Not just dozing on a couch!'

Robert opened one eye. 'I don't know. Two – maybe three days.'

'But why?' Julie put her hands on her hips. 'Surely you could have arranged things better than that.'

'What's the point of going to bed and tossing and turning for hours because you can't sleep?' he demanded harshly.

'That's nonsense! You're exhausted.'

Robert sighed, and rolling over reached for the aspirins.

Dropping three into the palm of his hand, he tossed them to the back of his throat and swallowed a mouthful of water to get rid of them, grimacing at the taste. Then he lay back on the cushions, looking up at her wearily.

'I'm sorry to be a nuisance,' he remarked sardonically.

Julie lifted her shoulders. 'You're not a nuisance!' she exclaimed. 'Why did you come here, Robert?'

He closed his eyes. 'I wanted to see you. Halbird said you'd rung this morning to speak to my mother when she wasn't at home. I thought maybe there was some kind of crisis for you to ring her.'

Julie bent her head. 'Oh, I see.'

He opened his eyes again. 'Was it important?'

'No. I wanted to talk to her about – about Sandra Lawson. I suppose you know she's here.' He nodded and she put a hand to her mouth. 'I suppose she knows I went out with Francis, too.'

Robert moved his head slowly from side to side, his eyes closed again. 'No, she doesn't. I arrived about nine-thirty, and I had plenty of opportunity to speak to Mrs. Hudson before Sandra arrived back.'

Julie frowned. 'And Pamela?'

'What about Pamela?' He sounded indifferent.

'Well, Sandra was having dinner with Pamela and her mother. Didn't you see her when she brought Sandra home?'

'No.' Robert was uncompromising.

Julie made a helpless gesture. 'But won't she think that's odd? I mean – your being here?'

Robert shrugged, opening his eyes again. 'Probably. But she knows better than to object.'

Julie sighed. 'And what did Sandra say when she saw you?'

'Hello.'

'Oh, you're being deliberately obtuse!' Julie would have

turned away, but he reached out and slid his fingers between hers and she halted reluctantly.

'No, I'm not,' he murmured huskily. 'I just don't want to talk about Pamela right now.'

Julie looked down at him uncertainly. 'Where did you tell Sandra I was?'

'*I* didn't. Mrs. Hudson explained that you had gone out for a while, and I think she was so astounded at seeing me, she couldn't think of anything to say.'

'I can believe that!' said Julie, with feeling.

He played with her fingers absently, his thumb massaging her palm. 'Do you want me to go?' His thick lashes successfully concealed the expression in his eyes.

Julie took a deep breath. 'You can't drive anywhere in that state!' she said firmly. 'You'll have to sleep here tonight.'

'Where? In your bed?' His fingers tightened on hers.

'Yes. My bed,' agreed Julie shortly, and pulled herself away from him. 'Can you make it upstairs?'

Robert regarded her in a strange way. 'I'm not an invalid, you know.'

'I know that.' Julie walked towards the door and looked back as he slid his legs to the ground and got to his feet. He flexed his back muscles tiredly and then she went out of the room and up the stairs without looking back.

In her room, she turned down the clean sheets which Mrs. Hudson had put there that morning, and removed her nightdress from under the pillow just as Robert appeared in the doorway. Despite his boast he looked pale and exhausted, and leaned negligently against the door jamb.

'You know where the bathroom is,' said Julie, moving away from the bed. 'Is there anything else you need?'

'Only you,' he muttered huskily. 'Come here.'

'Not now.' Julie evaded his reaching hands and made for the door. 'Get into bed.'

He began to unbutton his shirt with a complete lack of modesty and Julie went hastily out of the room, closing the door behind her. Then she heaved a deep breath and walked a little way along the landing to Emma's room.

The child was sleeping soundly, and Julie let herself into the room silently and quickly took off her clothes, slipping the nightdress over her head. Then she slid into the big bed beside Emma, moving her daughter over a little and allowing her to nestle closer to her.

'Mummy?' murmured Emma sleepily, her small hands questing over Julie's face.

Julie drew them down and squeezed them. 'Yes, Mummy,' she reassured her quietly. 'Go to sleep!'

Julie slept late the next morning, and so did Emma. She was not accustomed to sleeping with anybody and consequently the warmth that Julie generated enveloped her in a cosy glow and she slept on and on.

Julie eventually awoke as her daughter was stirring, and smiled sleepily at her astonished little face.

'Why are you sleeping with me?' she demanded, in surprise.

Julie stretched. 'Do you mind?'

'No. But why?'

Julie slid out of bed, glancing in amazement at her watch. It was after ten o'clock. 'Because I let someone else sleep in my bed,' she said.

'Who?' Emma looked excited.

'Uncle Robert,' replied Julie, yawning, and walking into the bathroom. When she returned a few minutes later, Emma was gone.

Sighing, Julie pulled on her dressing-gown. She had no illusions as to where Emma might be. She only hoped she would be in time to stop her from waking Robert up if he was still asleep.

However, when she reached her room, the door was pulled closed and when she looked inside she found Emma nowhere to be seen. Only Robert was stretched out in the bed, the bedcovers pushed down to his waist, his chest bare, sound asleep.

Julie's lips tilted slightly. There was a painful kind of ecstasy just seeing him there, in her bed, so relaxed and at peace. She was tempted to linger, but remembering what had happened last night she went out again and closed the door silently.

Downstairs, Emma was in the kitchen with Mrs. Hudson, who was grumbling away to herself as she prepared a tray. Julie frowned. 'What's going on?'

Mrs. Hudson looked at her resignedly. 'Your Miss Lawson appeared in here half an hour ago demanding to know why breakfast hadn't been prepared. I explained that you didn't normally get up particularly early, and that as you'd been out last night ...' She sighed. 'Anyway, the upshot of it was that she said she always ate a good breakfast, and would I supply her with a tray of cereal, bacon, eggs, toast and coffee!'

Julie endeavoured to smooth her tangled hair. She had not had time to comb it yet. 'I see.' She glanced at her daughter. 'Did you go into Uncle Robert's room?'

Emma looked downcast for a moment. 'Yes. But he was asleep, so I crept out again. Did I wake him up?'

'Fortunately not,' said Julie reprovingly, and then realized that Mrs. Hudson was staring at her in astonishment.

'Did Mr. Robert sleep here last night?'

Julie coloured. 'I'm afraid so. He was exhausted. He was asleep when I got home.'

Mrs. Hudson nodded 'Yes, I know. He apparently arrived back from New York only about seven-thirty last evening, and then after visiting his apartment he drove on down here'.

'Yes.' Julie tightened the cord of her pale blue housecoat. 'I expect you were surprised to see him.'

'Yes, ma'am. Not that I minded. It was company, like. And then after Miss Lawson went to bed he said he'd wait up for you.' She searched Julie's face. 'You – you didn't mind me going to bed?'

'Heavens, no!' Julie smiled and Mrs. Hudson looked relieved.

'There,' she said, adding a plate of ham and eggs and tomato to the already loaded tray. 'I'll just take this up to her.'

Julie frowned. 'You mean she's gone back to bed?'

'Oh, I don't know about that, ma'am, but she said she'd be in her room.'

'I see.' Julie bit her lip. 'Well, give it to me. I've got to go up to get dressed. I'll take it to her.' She looked down at Emma. 'You can have your cereal in here, can't you?'

Emma nodded and Julie took the tray firmly from the housekeeper and opening the door made her way back upstairs.

As she had suspected, Sandra Lawson was dressed and seated by her dressing-table apparently writing letters. She looked up in surprise when Julie made her entrance.

'Thank you,' she said, making room on the side table for the tray. 'But Mrs. Hudson could have brought it up.'

'It's not part of Mrs. Hudson's duties to be chambermaid,' replied Julie shortly. 'And I was coming upstairs anyway.'

'Well, thank you, Mrs. Pemberton.' Sandra's smile was frozen.

Julie moved towards the door, aware of the other girl's appraising stare. She was obviously comparing Julie's tumbled loveliness with her own ordered appearance.

'By the way,' she said, as Julie was going out of the door,

'did you know that Mr. Pemberton was coming here last night?'

'Robert?' Julie thrust her hands into the pockets of her housecoat. 'No, I didn't know.'

Sandra frowned. 'I didn't hear his car leave. Was he still here when you got home?'

'Yes.' Julie took hold of the door handle. 'Actually, he didn't leave. He slept here!' And let her make what she likes of that, she thought childishly, closing the door with a definite click behind her.

Sandra had gone for a walk round the village and Emma was playing in the frost-frozen garden when Robert eventually appeared. Julie was in the kitchen, helping Mrs. Hudson prepare the vegetables for lunch when he opened the door. It was almost twelve, and he had obviously slept well, for his face had lost that haggard appearance it had had the night before. But what Julie was not prepared for was the hostile gleam in his eyes as he looked at her. Then he switched his attention to the housekeeper. 'Is it too late to beg a cup of coffee?'

Mrs. Hudson wiped her hands dry. 'Of course not. My, you look more – rested this morning.'

'Yes, I feel it.' Robert had to look at Julie then. 'Good morning Julie.'

'Good morning.' Julie's lips were tight.

He nodded again at Mrs. Hudson and disappeared. Julie found she was breathing rather quickly.

'Are you going to take it through to him, or shall I?' Mrs. Hudson had prepared a small tray with cups, coffee pot, sugar and cream. There were some scones, too, hot from the oven, oozing with butter and jam.

Julie pressed her lips together, looking down at her apron-covered denim slacks and flour-smudged blue jersey. 'I look such a sight,' she began, when Mrs. Hudson thrust the tray into her hands.

'Go along with you. You know you want to.'

Robert was in the lounge. He was standing by the window. In his formal grey town suit, with only the growth of a night's beard on his chin to indicate that he had not been home, he looked wholly unapproachable. He turned when he heard her entrance, and said: 'Thank you. I'll get away as soon as I've had this.'

Julie put down the tray. 'Would you like me to pour for you?'

He shrugged. 'If you like.'

Julie seated herself on the edge of the couch and tackled the cups. When his was poured she handed him the cup and offered the sugar basin. Robert helped himself to sugar and then raised the cup to his lips.

'I suppose I should apologize for the inconvenience,' he said bleakly.

'What inconvenience?' Julie rose to her feet again. She couldn't bear to feel at more of a disadvantage than she already was. 'You know I asked you to stay.' She looked up at him. 'Did you sleep well?'

He bit off an expletive. 'You know I did.'

Julie bent her head. 'Good.'

'Where did you sleep?'

'With Emma.'

'I see.' He finished his coffee and thrust down the cup. 'I must go. I apologize again for putting you out.'

'But you didn't!' exclaimed Julie unhappily.

At that moment Emma came running into the room. 'Uncle Robert! Uncle Robert!' she cried, and flung herself into his arms. Then she frowned. 'You're not leaving!'

'I'm afraid so.'

'But why? Mummy, why? Does he have to go?'

'I think so, darling.' Julie's throat was constricted.

Robert hugged the little girl. 'I'll come and see you again soon.'

Emma's mouth drooped. 'Oh, Uncle Robert, *please*! I came to your bedroom this morning, but Mummy wouldn't let me wake you. And now you're going!'

Robert frowned. 'I'm sure now that Miss Lawson's here—'

'Bother Miss Lawson. I don't like her!'

Emma pursed her lips and as she did so Julie became aware that Sandra was standing silently in the doorway watching them. Robert noticed her, too, and managed a polite: 'Good morning, Miss Lawson.'

Sandra Lawson's lips thinned. She must have heard what Emma had said, but she was going to ignore it, at least for the time being. 'Good morning, Mr. Pemberton. I've been for a walk round the village. Getting my bearings, as it were. It's cold, but quite exhilarating!'

'I'm sure it must be.' Robert smiled faintly.

Sandra smiled, too, and then turned her attention to Emma. 'And what have you been doing?'

'Nothing.' Emma was mutinous. Julie had never seen her this way before. The child was looking desperately up at Robert and there were tears sparkling on her long lashes. 'Please, Uncle Robert, don't go!'

Robert hesitated, glancing awkwardly at Julie. She made a helpless gesture. 'Stay if you'd like to.'

'Yes, do stay,' said Sandra unexpectedly. 'Actually, I thought you would, so I telephoned Pamela while I was out and asked her to come over.'

Julie gasped. 'You did what!'

'Cool it, Julie!' Robert was unperturbed. 'You told Pamela I was here?'

Sandra looked coy. 'No, not that. I thought it would be a nice surprise for her.'

Robert wiped a tear from Emma's cheek and there was a curious smile on his face now. 'I imagine you thought your actions would cause no little consternation here, Miss

136

Lawson,' he said, in an almost conversational voice.

Sandra coloured defensively. 'Pamela's my friend. I just did what I thought was best.'

'Best for whom? For Pamela? Or for you?'

'What do you mean?'

Robert looked at her squarely. 'What a petty little mind you have, Miss Lawson. Do you really imagine that when Pamela arrives and finds me here it will make the slightest difference to our relationship?'

'Of course—'

'Oh, no, Miss Lawson, it won't. Pamela is not exactly the sort of person you think she is. She wants to marry me because I'm entirely suitable, both socially and financially. The fact that I might stray now and then from the straight and narrow means little more than a mild annoyance to her. By telephoning her and bringing her here, all you will achieve is her humiliation. Do you think she'll thank you for that?'

Sandra uttered an exclamation. 'How can you stand there and admit such a thing—'

'I'm admitting nothing. I've got nothing to confess. Nor has Mrs. Pemberton, I might add.'

'What's going on, Uncle Robert?' Emma was getting impatient.

'Nothing, honey,' he replied, looking down at her gently. 'You go and take off your outdoor things and in five minutes I'll give you a game of snakes and ladders.'

'Super!' Emma scampered excitedly out of the room and Robert turned back to the governess.

'Well?'

Sandra moved uncomfortably, casting a malevolent glance in Julie's direction. 'It's too late now,' she said. 'I've made the phone call.'

Robert's expression was hard. 'Pamela is not to know the exact time I arrived. She isn't expecting me back until this evening. If she comes and finds me here this morning it will be a simple matter to pretend I arrived a short while ago, on my way to see her.' He rubbed his hand over the growth of beard on his chin. 'I can use the battery-operated shaver I have in the car. No one would be any the wiser.'

'You're actually asking me to assist your intrigue!' cried Sandra in horror.

'Not at all. All you're being asked to do is save Pamela from embarrassment.'

'But if she doesn't care where you – where you sleep – what does it matter?' she demanded triumphantly.

Robert's lips twisted. 'But you rang her, Miss Lawson. You deliberately set wheels in motion to bring her here and find me in residence. Do you think she'll find it easy to forgive you for that?'

'You – you're despicable!' Sandra bent her head, obviously having an inward battle with herself.

'Just practical,' remarked Robert coldly. 'Well?'

Sandra's face contorted. 'Very well, I'll say nothing. But I shan't forget this.'

'Nor shall I,' replied Robert heavily, and strode out of the room in search of Emma.

Julie sank down weakly on to the arm of a chair. She felt weak. It had all been too much for her, and she wished desperately that they would all go away and leave her and Emma alone. Robert's enmity this morning was destructive, particularly after his momentary tenderness last night.

Sandra was regarding her contemptuously. 'I suppose this is all for your benefit, isn't it?' she demanded.

Julie looked up wearily. 'What?'

'This elaborate charade! This pretence of just arriving back from the States! He's not concerned about Pamela being embarrassed or even that I might lose Pamela's friendship! All that concerns him is protecting you! Your reputation!' Her lips curled. 'I wonder why? Do you suppose he's afraid you're going to get your claws into him for a second time, and this time he might not get away scot-free?'

CHAPTER NINE

THINGS settled down to something like normal the following week, but then anything would have seemed like normal after the unpleasant tensions of Sunday. Only Emma had seemed unaware of the atmosphere, and perhaps Pamela, for she had accepted Robert's explanations without question.

But Julie had found it terribly difficult to behave naturally. Her nerves were stretched unbearably, and although Sandra behaved with admirable restraint, Julie could not relax.

After lunch, a meal throughout which Pamela had done most of the talking, Sandra suggested they might all go for a walk round the village, but Robert declined, so Pamela had asked Julie whether they might use the lounge for a while.

Julie had been only too pleased to agree, but later, as she sat with Mrs. Hudson in the kitchen, drinking her coffee, she saw Robert in the garden with Emma and realized the two women were alone.

Not that Robert seemed concerned. The ground was still diamond hard with frost and he and Emma were sliding down the path with apparently carefree abandon. But then Robert lost his balance and crashed to the ground with a thump.

Julie jumped to her feet, a hand to her mouth, and Mrs. Hudson looked out knowingly. 'He'll be all right,' she assured her, and as though to prove the point Emma straddled him excitedly, pressing his chest back against the path and sitting on it, while he protested laughingly. 'You see!' said Mrs. Hudson. 'You worry too much.' She shook her head cheerfully. 'She needs a father, and no mistake.'

Julie sighed. 'I expect she misses Michael.'

Mrs. Hudson hunched her shoulders. 'Happen she does,' she said, but she didn't sound convinced.

Pamela and Robert left soon afterwards, driving away in their separate cars, bound for Pamela's parents' home at Orpington. Sandra waved them off, but Julie kept out of the way. She wondered how Robert would react to Francis now.

During the next few days, Emma started her lessons with Sandra. The girl had brought some textbooks and paper with her, sufficient to last them for the first couple of weeks, and she told Julie indifferently that if Emma progressed satisfactorily she would send to London for more.

But Emma did not progress satisfactorily. From being a good-natured, mild-tempered little girl, she became a stormy, tearful tyrant, and even Julie had to reprove her.

'I can't understand it,' she said to Mrs. Hudson one afternoon. 'She used to say she wanted to go to school.'

'Having a governess isn't the same as going to school,' said Mrs. Hudson in her calm, practical way. 'The little one has no friends. She doesn't get a chance to associate with other children, and she's lonely. And she knows so long as Miss Lawson stays here, she'll stay that way.'

'But Robert won't agree to anything else!' exclaimed Julie exasperatedly, her own troubles swamped by her anxiety over her daughter.

'What about Mrs. Pemberton?' suggested Mrs. Hudson, frowning.

'Oh, she'd never agree with me! Besides, Sandra is a friend of the family.'

Mrs. Hudson shook her head. 'So what are you going to do?'

'I don't know. I honestly don't know.'

'What about Mr. Hillingdon? Couldn't he talk to Mr.

Robert? Maybe he'd listen to him.'

Julie grimaced. 'I doubt that. I doubt that very much.'

The housekeeper sighed. 'Well, I don't know what else you can do. But something will have to be done, for the lassie is crying herself to sleep nights.'

'I know.' Julie sighed, now. 'And Sandra keeps complaining to me about her rudeness in lessons. I'm sure she'd like to slap her.'

'Yes, well, I'm sure the feeling's mutual,' remarked Mrs. Hudson dryly.

'I'm sure it is.' Julie tugged worriedly at a strand of her hair. 'All right, I'll ring Francis.'

She got through to him at the office. He sounded delighted to hear from her as usual. 'When am I going to see you again?'

Julie lifted her shoulders helplessly. 'Actually, Francis, it's your help I want.'

'Help? In what way?' Francis sounded surprised.

'I want you to speak to Robert. To ask him whether he would reconsider his decision concerning Emma's schooling. She wants to go to the village school, and she simply won't behave. Sandra's been marvellously patient with her in the circumstances.'

'I see.' Francis expelled his breath noisily. 'Would you like me to come and talk to Emma herself?'

'I don't think that would do any good. She'd be delighted to see you, of course, but after you'd gone ...' Her voice trailed away.

'Yes, I see what you mean.' Francis sounded thoughtful. 'But I ought to tell you that Robert and I don't seem on the best of terms at the moment. He – well, last Sunday when he came over, he made some pretty rough remarks to me when we were having a drink together before dinner.'

Julie gasped. 'What about?'

'Can't you guess? You, of course. He told me to leave you

alone – that he found my behaviour disgusting – and that he wasn't going to stand by and let you ruin your life. You know the sort of thing.'

Julie was horrified. 'Oh, I'm sorry.'

Francis made an amused snort. 'Yes, well, I was pretty mad myself at the time, but then afterwards I realized he was only talking in your best interests. He seems to feel a strong sense of responsibility for you – for you both. I don't know how his marriage to Pamela is going to stand up in the face of such a commitment.'

'What do you mean?' Julie was trembling.

'Well, if I didn't know him better, I'd say he felt more than a moral obligation towards you. But that's ridiculous, isn't it? After all, he called off your wedding, didn't he?'

'Y–e–s.' Julie bit her lower lip, finding it difficult to concentrate on the real reason she had rung Francis in the first place. 'But – will you speak to him?'

Francis hesitated. 'If it's what you want,' he said, at last.

'It is.'

'Right. He's coming to lunch tomorrow. I'll try and have a word with him then.'

'Oh, thank you, Francis. Thank you.'

'Don't thank me yet. I haven't achieved anything.'

Mrs. Hudson was pleased when Julie told her what she had done. 'Mr Hillingdon has a persuasive way with him, as you should know,' she commented dryly.

Julie smiled slightly. 'Yes. But apparently Robert has taken him to task for taking me out last week-end and they're not on such good terms as they were.'

The housekeeper raised her eyebrows. 'Indeed?' She smiled. 'Well, well.'

Julie looked sharply at her. 'What do you mean? Well, well?'

Mrs. Hudson shook her head, studying the balance of the

scales as she weighed out the ingredients for the cake she was making. 'It's nothing to do with me, Mrs. Pemberton.'

'You can't say that, having already commented.' Julie perched on the high stool. 'Oh, if only Robert will agree to Emma attending the village school. She'll make some friends of her own age—'

'And yon governess will be out of the house!'

'That, of course,' agreed Julie, sighing. 'I can't understand Emma. She's always been so good before.'

Mrs. Hudson sieved flour into a basin. 'I expect having her grandmother and Mr. Robert and that Mr. Hillingdon making a fuss of her has gone to her head. She's only five years old, Mrs. Pemberton. And just think of the changes of circumstances she's had to adapt to during the last few months!'

'Do you think she's spoilt, then?' Julie was concerned.

'Bless you, no! She could do with a bit of spoiling, if you ask me. No, it's just she's trying to find her feet and there've been so many people around.'

'Do you think that's why she makes such a fuss of Robert when he comes?'

Mrs. Hudson pulled a wry face. 'Not altogether. I think she sees him as a kind of security, of course, but it's more than that I think. She seems – well, attached to him. She's always talking about him, you know. She talks about Mr. Hillingdon, too, of course, but Mr. Robert's her favourite.'

Julie pressed her palms to her cheeks, feeling the unwelcome prick of tears behind her eyes. 'I see.'

'He would be, wouldn't he, Mrs. Pemberton?' Mrs. Hudson spoke in such a low voice that Julie scarcely heard what she said.

'What was that?' she asked.

Mrs. Hudson coloured now. 'I said – well, he would be

her favourite, wouldn't he?'

'Why?' Julie's voice was jerky.

'Well, being Mr. Michael's brother and all, and looking like him.'

'Oh, I see what you mean.' Julie sounded relieved.

'What did you think I meant?'

Julie made a helpless movement of her shoulders. 'Why – nothing.'

Mrs. Hudson wiped her floury hands on her apron. 'You should have married Mr. Robert, ma'am. Then he'd have been Emma's father, wouldn't he?'

Julie stared at her. 'It wasn't to be,' she said tightly.

'No. Because you wouldn't marry him before he left for Venezuela, would you, ma'am?'

'How do you know that?'

Mrs. Hudson sighed. 'Mr. Robert told me, the other evening. We were talking about the days when he used to go on those assignments.'

'I see.' Julie slid off the stool. 'What – what else did he say?'

'Nothing much. Just that you'd been upset about him going.'

Julie bent her head. 'That's not unnatural.'

'You could have gone with him, as his wife.'

'I know.' Julie felt frozen inside. 'But we had a row...'

'About him going just a week before the wedding?'

'Yes. Oh, I realize it was stupid now, but at the time it seemed important.' She sighed. 'I was only nineteen.'

Mrs. Hudson measured out some sugar. 'And afterwards?'

Julie made an impatient gesture. 'What's the use of dredging it up now? No good can come of talking about it.'

'It sometimes does you good to talk,' remarked Mrs. Hudson quietly, 'and from the way you're acting now, I shouldn't think you've talked about this much.'

'Only to Michael,' murmured Julie reminiscently.

Mrs. Hudson nodded. 'I see.'

Julie heaved a sigh. 'Did Robert tell you what happened the night we split up?'

'No.' Mrs. Hudson began beating up some eggs. 'Can you imagine Mr. Robert confiding his troubles to me?'

Julie tugged at a strand of her hair. 'Not really.'

'Tell me how you got to know him.'

Julie shrugged. 'I worked for the company. My boss introduced us, actually. I had heard of Robert, of course. He had quite a reputation.'

'And?'

'I wanted nothing to do with him. I wasn't — well, that kind of a girl, to coin an old-fashioned phrase.'

'I see.' Mrs. Hudson's smile was gentle. 'Go on.'

Julie grimaced. 'Oh, well, Robert was very insistent. He used to make excuses to come to Mr. Harvey's office where I worked; he'd offer to drive me home, take me out to lunch, that sort of thing. The other girls used to warn me about him, but it wasn't necessary. I already knew what he was like. He was used to getting his own way. But he didn't try anything after the first time.' She sighed. 'I thought that would be that, but it wasn't. He asked me to marry him!' She shook her head helplessly. 'I couldn't believe it. I thought it was some kind of elaborate ploy to get me to go to bed with him. But it wasn't.'

'And then what happened?'

'The usual things. He took me to meet his mother. She had a house in Richmond in those days — oh, of course, you'd know that. Well, anyway, she never liked me, but I think she realized that Robert was serious and therefore she'd have to make the best of it. And all the arrangements for the wedding were made. I was brought up in a children's home. My parents were killed in a car crash, and I was an orphan, so I had nobody to arrange things. Mrs. Pemberton dealt with everything. Then the Venezuela job exploded!'

'And it was all off?'

'Yes.'

Julie turned away. She didn't want to talk about it any more. It was all too painful to remember even now. Mrs. Hudson, with her innate perceptiveness, realized Julie's dilemma and changed the subject, and Julie was grateful to her.

But later that evening, when Julie was in the bath, the conversation came back to her and with it the realization that no matter what happened now she would always regret the past.

Soaping her legs, she recalled the events of that evening, the evening Robert had to tell her that he was having to go to Venezuela to take charge of the Guaba project.

But he hadn't told her at the beginning of the evening. They had met in town as usual, and had dinner together at one of the small intimate restaurants they favoured. If Robert had seemed a little silent and morose Julie had scarcely noticed it, too happy and excited at the knowledge that in exactly a week she would be Mrs. Robert Pemberton.

But when the meal was over she had had to acknowledge that something was wrong. A twinge of fear had touched her heart, and when Robert had suggested they should drive down to his mother's house in Richmond Julie had agreed, wondering whether, despite everything that had been arranged, this was the moment when it was all going to be called off.

In the car she had searched her thoughts, trying to find some incident, some disagreement in her memory which might have led to this disturbing state of affairs. But there was nothing. She must be wrong, she told herself, to become alarmed unnecessarily.

The house Robert shared with his mother in Richmond

was comfortably large, a family house, set in its own grounds, with tennis courts and a pool out back. It was the house Robert's father had had built for his own use, and both Robert and Michael had been brought up there. Julie had visited it only seldom. Lucy Pemberton was always in residence and Julie knew she was not ever really welcome. That was what made it so strange that Robert should be taking her there this evening.

However, when the car drew to a halt at the front door, she saw the house was in darkness and looked inquiringly at Robert.

'My mother's away for the week-end,' he explained, sliding out of the car and walking round to help her out.

Julie got out reluctantly. 'Why have you brought me here, Robert?'

Robert slammed her door. 'Come on in. I could do with a drink.'

Inside the comfortably furnished hall, he closed the door and led the way into the lounge. As he did so, Mrs. Hughes, his mother's housekeeper, appeared from the kitchen and looked in some surprise at them.

'I thought you were staying in town this evening, sir,' she commented queryingly.

'I was.' Robert was abrupt. 'Don't alarm yourself, Mrs. Hughes. We shan't require anything. You can go.'

'Yes, sir.' Mrs. Hughes had looked doubtfully at Julie before going out and closing the door behind her with obvious disapproval.

Julie stood behind the couch, watching Robert pour himself a Scotch, and then he turned irritably and said: 'Take off your coat. Sit down. We shan't be disturbed.'

'Why have you brought me here?' Julie was concerned and couldn't hide it.

Robert's expression softened. 'Don't look so alarmed, Julie. I wanted to talk to you somewhere where I knew we shouldn't be disturbed, that's all. Come and sit down, please.'

Julie unbuttoned her coat and taking it off laid it across the back of a chair. Then she came round and seated herself on the soft brocade-covered couch.

'Do you want a drink?' Robert indicated the bottles.

'No, thanks.' Julie shook her head. She wished he would say what he had to say and be done with it. Whatever it was!

Robert seemed to sense her misgivings and came to stand on the hearth before her, looking down at her with those intense grey eyes of his. It made her want to stand up and wrap her arms around him, she badly needed to feel the warmth of his reassurance, but until she knew why he had brought her here she was constrained.

At last he said: 'I've had some bad news, Julie.'

'Bad news!' Julie felt a cold hand squeeze her heart. 'What kind of bad news? It – it's not Michael, is it?' At that time Michael was abroad with his ship and for a moment she thought he might have been injured or even killed.

Robert shook his head, however, relieving her of that anxiety only to replace it with another. 'No, it's not Michael. Moran was killed in Venezuela yesterday.'

Julie had a hand to her throat, but now her brows drew together in puzzlement. 'Moran?' she echoed. 'You mean – Dennis Moran?' Dennis Moran was an engineering consultant working for the Pemberton company. She had met him once or twice at the office, but she hardly knew him and certainly had no idea where he might be working at the moment.

'That's right,' Robert was saying now. 'He was working on the Guaba river valley project.' He considered a moment. 'Have you heard of it?'

'Vaguely.' Julie tried to think. 'Wasn't that the project you began initially?'

'That's right.' Robert nodded.

Julie made an expressive movement of her shoulders. 'Even so – well, I'm sorry, naturally, but apart from the fact that the death of any individual is distressing, I don't see how—'

'You don't see how it affects us? Is that it?' Robert's face was sombre.

'Well, yes.' Julie swallowed hard. 'Is – is that all?'

'I'm afraid not.' Robert heaved a sigh. 'This project is already overdue. The rains are expected soon and the dam has to be in position before then.'

Julie held her breath. 'So?'

Robert uttered an expletive. 'You're not making it very easy for me, Julie.'

'What do you want me to say?' Julie stared at him. 'I don't see how this man's death affects us!'

'Don't you? Or don't you want to see?' Robert turned away, resting his arm on the mantelpiece and leaning his head on his arm. 'Surely it's obvious,' he went on in a muffled voice. 'I've got to go out there and supervise the completion of the work!'

Julie got to her feet then. 'You've got to go to Venezuela?' she exclaimed, in dismay.

'That's right.'

'But why you?' For the moment Julie had forgotten the wedding only days away.

'Because, as you so accurately put it a few moments ago, I began the work initially. Moran took over from me.'

Julie shook her head. 'But even so, there must be other engineers—' She broke off suddenly. 'What does this mean? What are you trying to say? When do you expect to leave?'

Robert turned back to her and his face was grim. 'I have to leave in – two, maybe three days—'

'But you can't!' Julie was horrified. 'Robert, have you for-

150

gotten—'

'For heaven's sake, how could I forget?' he muttered fiercely. 'That's why I brought you here, isn't it? That's why I'm telling you straight out. I want you to try and understand my position—'

'*Your* position!' cried Julie. 'What about my position?' She made a helpless gesture. 'You can't do this. Why can't someone else go? Why does it have to be you?'

Robert made a calming movement with his hands. 'Cool down, Julie,' he said heavily. 'Try and look at the situation logically. Do you suppose I *want* to go to Venezuela?'

'I don't know what you want,' snapped Julie chokily. 'I – I can't think straight.'

Robert sighed. 'Of course you know what I want,' he bit out harshly. 'I want to stay here, I want to be with you, I want to marry you! I've wanted you long enough. How do you think I feel?'

Julie moved her head disbelievingly. 'I don't think anything any more,' she exclaimed. 'Go on! You haven't given me the excuse why you have to go.'

'Damn you, it's not an excuse,' snapped Robert. 'It's a reason! Look, I'll try to make it clearer for you. As I've said, I did the ground work for this project. It was my design, my baby. When everything seemed to be going smoothly, Moran took over. But for some inexplicable reason, there's been an explosion at the dam, and Moran's been killed. How the hell could I send someone out there to investigate knowing full well it was my responsibility to do so?'

Julie linked and unliked her fingers. 'But, Robert, this is no ordinary time. Heavens, everything's arranged for next week. We can't just call it off.'

'I'm not suggesting we call it off,' said Robert, in a dangerously hostile tone. 'All I want is for you to agree to a postponement.'

'A postponement!' Julie chewed her lips nervously. 'And

how do you suppose people will take that?'

'What do you mean?'

'Exactly what I say.' She shook her head. 'Can't you see? Are you so blind, too? The fact that you're leaving on this assignment will be proof to them that we're through – finished! That the postponement is simply the overture to the cancellation!'

'Stop talking nonsense!' Robert was impatient, his own nerves strung up at this unexpected intrusion into his plans. 'It needn't be a long postponement, a month – maybe two.'

'*Two months!*' Julie turned away. 'Let someone else go.'

'I can't.' He was adamant. 'Julie, I've tried to explain. If you don't believe me, I don't know what else I can say.'

Julie bent her head. 'How can I believe you? Does your mother know about this?'

'Yes, she knows.'

'I expect she was jubilant,' murmured Julie bitterly. 'After all, it gives her a few more weeks to persuade you you're making the biggest mistake of your life, doesn't it?'

'*Julie!*' Robert's tone was agonized, and he put his hands on her shoulders trying to turn her towards him, but she shrugged him off, moving out of his reach.

'Don't touch me!' she cried.

Robert caught his breath angrily. 'Julie, you're being ridiculous! You're behaving as though I'm trying to back out of the wedding.'

'And aren't you?'

'*No!*' The word was a fierce repudiation, but Julie was too miserable to think coherently.

'I want to go home,' she said dully.

'Julie!' He was exasperated. 'You can't go like this. We haven't finished talking about it. There are arrangements to be made about sending out postponement notices—'

'I want to go home!' Julie repeated, turning on him. 'You make what arrangements you like. It's nothing to do with me, anyway. Your mother arranged it all.'

Robert raked a hand through his hair. 'I won't let you go like this,' he groaned. 'Julie, be sensible! I love you. Doesn't that mean anything any more?'

'Apparently not,' said Julie scornfully.

'What do you mean?'

'If you loved me, you couldn't do this to me – to us!' Julie stared appealing at him. 'Robert, please, let someone else go. Peters, perhaps. Or – or Lionel Grant.'

'No.' Robert was adamant. 'Julie, I've got to go. Accept it!'

'Never!' Julie was becoming emotional, and although she knew she might regret such an ultimatum in the cold light of morning, right now all she could think of was that she was not going to be able to walk down the aisle of St. Margaret's on Saturday wearing the gorgeous lace gown Robert's mother had had made for her, carrying a bouquet of white roses, or depart on that exotic honeymoon in the Caribbean. It was childish, but compared to Robert she was a child – then.

Robert looked about him rather desperately, as though seeking for words to substantiate his claim. 'Julie, you can't do this to me,' he said, rather huskily. 'I – well – God, I need you!'

'Do you?' she taunted him. 'You'd never know it.'

'What do you mean?' He glared at her.

Julie shook her head. 'Oh, nothing.' She was already beginning to realize that Robert was almost at the end of his tether, too. She walked to the door. 'I want to go home. Will you take me, or do I have to walk to the railway station and take a train?'

Robert stood regarding her with brooding animosity. 'You're not leaving yet,' he announced grimly. 'As I said earlier, there are arrangements to be made.'

'Not so far as I'm concerned,' retorted Julie, reaching for her coat and sliding her arms into it.

Robert moved then, his anger erupting into action. He caught her by her upper arms, wrenching her body close up against his, so that she could feel every hard muscle straining against hers. Then he bent his head and fastened his mouth to hers in a kiss that was as brutal as it was unexpected. And yet in spite of that, the urgent response it aroused in Julie's body could not be denied, and her lips parted weakly.

When he eventually lifted his head she did not notice the strain in his face, only the coldness in his eyes. 'Well?' he demanded, 'now tell me you won't marry me!'

Julie stared back at him. She ached to admit that he was right, that she would wait for him for as long as he wanted her to, but the utter contempt in his voice destroyed these admissions at birth. Instead, she struggled impotently with him, trying to free herself, trying to draw up her fists and hammer that contempt from his lean dark face.

'No, I won't marry you!' she exclaimed fiercely. 'I – I hate you!'

Robert's eyes darkened and he put a rough hand behind her head and brought her mouth to his again, his kiss more savage and brutal than the last, conveying his anger and contempt at his own need of her.

But Julie didn't sense that immediately. To her it was simply a case of his taking out his anger on her, and although the continued insistence of his lovemaking was seductive, she tried desperately to fight back.

It was a losing battle. Robert was so much stronger than she was for one thing, and he was an expert when it came to getting what he wanted from a woman. He had never used that expertise on Julie before, respecting her innocence, prepared to wait until she was his wife and free to love him without restraint. But now he had been driven beyond the limits of his endurance. He had never kissed her so deeply, so intimately, sliding the coat from her shoulders to fall unresistingly in a heap at her feet, caressing her so that a flame started in her veins and ran to the extremities of her body. It was like drowning, she thought, in one of her more coherent moments, and while an escape to the surface might be safer there was something infinitely desirable about giving in and allowing the tide of emotion to sweep over her...

Now, Julie climbed out of the bath and began to dry herself. Recalling that evening six years ago had made her restless and she could not relax any longer.

She was beginning to realize that she had been as much to blame for what had happened as Robert. But at the time, she had blamed it all on him and had refused to listen when he had attempted to apologize. Apologies were little consolation for the enormity of his crime, and she had behaved without reason, running from the house as though the devil himself was at her heels.

There had been pitifully few days left for Robert to make amends, days when he should have been making his own arrangements for departure. Lucy Pemberton herself had even gone to Julie in an effort to avert the disastrous effect Julie's attitude was having on her son, but Julie wouldn't listen to her. She didn't want to hear about postponements, about wedding presents that she felt sure would never now be hers, and Lucy had left her in high dudgeon, blaming the whole sorry affair on her.

Eventually, Robert himself came to her flat. She had left her job at the office the week previously and she had known he would have to come in search of her if he wanted to persuade her that anything was different from what she believed. She still clung to the idea that he might give up this plan to go to Venezuela, but his words when she opened the door to him disabused her of that supposition.

He had been brief and almost formal in his approach, only the lines of fatigue around his eyes and beside his mouth bearing witness to his own mental state. He had suggested that they got married immediately, in a register office. There was nothing to stop them, and once she had had the necessary inoculations and injections she could follow him out to Venezuela.

But to Julie that had been the last straw. She had seen it as his attempt to make amends for the fact that he had made love to her, and she became convinced in her own mind that without that guilt on his conscience he would never have made such a suggestion. Why hadn't he asked her to marry him the night he told her of the proposed assignment? Why had he waited until now?

The row that followed was brief, too, but explosive, and after he had gone she had known that she had destroyed everything between them by her own stubborn obstinacy.

She had thought that that would be the end of it. She had read about Robert's departure for Venezuela in the paper and the brief comment that his wedding had had to be postponed because of his business commitments, but she had known that had been only a face-saver so far as Lucy Pemberton was concerned. She thought she would never see either Robert or his family again. But she had been wrong.

In the first few weeks following Robert's departure she had managed to find another secretarial post in order to support herself, avoiding any coffee bars or restaurants where she might conceivably run into any of the crowd from the Pemberton building. She couldn't face them; not yet. Life assumed a kind of routine and she blunted the pain of her separation from Robert by spending all her evenings at concerts or at the cinema so that when she arrived back at the flat she was too exhausted to do anything but go to bed.

Surprisingly, she slept quite well, and initially she put this down to nervous exhaustion. But later, as the weeks went by, the realization of what was happening to her became apparent. Even then, she wouldn't accept it, convincing herself that the events of the past few weeks had simply upset her normal metabolism. It wasn't until she began to feel nauseated when she got up in the morning and could no longer face the smell of strong coffee that she had to acknowledge that she was pregnant.

She panicked, naturally. She had no parents, no one to whom she could turn. She had heard of societies that helped people in her condition, but she dreaded contacting one of them. She dreaded having to supply some stranger with all the details and watch them looking at her with unconcealed pity.

No, rather she should face Robert with this knowledge and allow him to pay for the birth and possible adoption. He might even want to keep the child himself. She would not consider the possibility that he might want her too.

So she wrote to Lucy Pemberton asking her if she would send her Robert's address in Venezuela. Lucy did not reply, but several days later Michael Pemberton visited her. He was home on leave from his ship, he told her, and as his mother was not well he had taken it upon himself to come and give her Robert's address. It wasn't until later that Julie learned that Lucy had forbidden him to contact her again.

Julie had spoken rather uncomfortably to Robert's brother, unable to relax in case he should suspect the motives behind her desiring to know Robert's whereabouts. And yet Michael had been quite kind, and he had tried to put her at her ease.

She wrote to Robert at once, not telling him of her condition, merely asking him whether it would be possible for him to fly to England and see her. She wanted to see his face when he received the news. It was not something one could baldly state in a letter which might fall into the wrong hands.

Robert's reply, however, was scarcely civil. He told her there was no possibility of his being able to return to England at this time, and that he expected to be away at least a further three months.

Julie was distrait. She didn't know where to turn next. And it was in this humiliatingly tearful state that she had opened the door one evening a few days after receiving Robert's letter and found Michael Pemberton again on the threshold.

If he had been bewildered by her obvious distress, he had contained his curiosity, and after she had admitted him he had made her sit down and calm herself while he made some tea. His compassion had been too much for Julie. With gentle encouragement she had poured out the whole story and he had listened intently to what she had to say. When she showed him Robert's letter, he suggested that she should write again and tell his brother the truth. He was convinced, he said, that had Robert suspected anything like this he would never have been so cold, so dismissive.

But Julie was adamant on that score. It was obvious, she said, that Robert was no longer interested in what happened to her, and if she were to write and tell him of her condition he would only come back out of decency, and not because he really wanted her.

Michael argued with her, but finally agreed that Robert should not hear any of this from him.

In the days that followed he was a frequent visitor at Julie's flat. Julie didn't mind. It gave her something else to think about, although she was sure his mother would not approve of this alliance. When he eventually proposed marriage, however, she was astounded. She had never dreamt that this might be in his mind, for although she had become fond of him, he was simply Robert's brother, not a personality in his own right.

Michael, though, proved to be a determined advocate of his cause. He had explained that through his connection with the Admiralty he had been offered a post in Rhatoon on the west coast of Malaya, and he was only hesitating about accepting it because he would be the only unmarried man among a group of married people. He explained the advantages and disadvantages of living out there, but his most persuasive theme was that Julie would be able to have the baby without anyone, least of all Robert, discovering that it was not Michael's child. The appointment was likely to be a lengthy one and probably by the time they returned to England Robert would be married himself and Julie would have forgotten this disastrous and unhappy affair. It was a great temptation, a wonderful opportunity to escape, not only from the consequences of her condition but also from the chance of Robert finding out that she had had a child and then demanding why he had not been informed.

From the distance of years Julie could see that like all her actions it had been motivated by an unreasoning sense of panic, a mindless cowardly desire to run and hide, to bury her head in the sand, and pretend that everything could be made right again. Maybe Michael had been partially to blame. He had provided her with this escape and once he saw she was weakening he had pressed his advantage at every opportunity until at least she gave in.

They were married a few days later in a register office with only two of Michael's friends as witnesses. Lucy Pemberton had taken another of her unwell attacks, but they both knew that in reality she had refused to come to the wedding. She couldn't understand why Michael should be foolish enough as to want to marry a woman of Julie's calibre, and she saw Julie's behaviour as a deliberate attempt to thwart the Pemberton family.

But they left for Rhatoon within a month of the wedding

and out there, away from the influence of the Pembertons, there was no one to view their marriage as anything less than a normal one. Julie had the baby in the spring and no one could have been more delighted with their daughter than Michael. It was not until Emma was three months old that he made any attempt to consummate their relationship, and by then Julie was so grateful to him for his generosity and understanding that it was almost easy to be kind to him; and if she never found with Michael the ecstasy she had known with Robert, she refused to put it down to anything more than the differences in their temperaments.

Now Julie viewed her reflection in the bathroom mirror without pleasure. Maybe she had made a terrible mistake all those years ago in believing that Robert thought more about his work than about her. Maybe he had had no choice in the matter of the explosion at Guaba. Certainly she had been fooling herself all those months and years in Rhatoon if she had ever succeeded in convincing herself that what she had felt for Robert had died. She had merely succeeded in burying it beneath a layer of bitterness, and who could have guessed, certainly not she, that Michael would die so tragically and thrust her back into the mêlée of the emotions he aroused in her.

CHAPTER TEN

THE following morning Sandra came into the kitchen soon after eleven looking furious.

'Something will have to be done about that child!' she declared. 'She's just upset my bottle of ink all over the textbook I was using.'

'Oh, heavens, I'm sorry!' Julie was apologetic. 'I'll speak to her at once.'

'Don't bother!' Sandra's lips curled. 'I've punished her myself.'

Mrs. Hudson looked up from her baking at this and Julie felt her nerves tighten. 'I see,' she said carefully. 'And what form did this punishment take?'

'I've cut down the swing.'

'You've done what?' Julie was horrified. She rushed to the window and looked out; the severed ropes on the cherry tree looked bleak and ominous in the grey light.

'It was the only way,' went on Sandra, self-righteously. 'Would you rather I'd spanked her?'

Julie shook her head slowly. 'No, I suppose not. But the swing – it was her favourite occupation.'

'Precisely. There was little point in depriving her of something she didn't value.'

Mrs. Hudson's mouth turned down at the corners, expressing her disapproval, but Julie was trying to be fair. After all, if Emma had overturned the bottle of ink deliberately then she did indeed deserve to be punished. Even so ...

'Er – where is she now, then?' Julie asked, endeavouring to appear calm.

Sandra shrugged. 'In her room, I imagine. I've dismissed

her for the rest of the morning.' She glanced round. 'Is there any coffee available? I'd like to take a cup up to my room. I have some letters to write and I might as well be doing them as wasting my time trying to educate a child who plainly doesn't wish to be educated!'

Julie controlled the impulse to retaliate and herself provided Sandra with a tray. After the governess had departed Mrs. Hudson viewed the broken swing with some misgivings.

'That was a spiteful thing to do, ma'am,' she exclaimed, obviously unable to suppress her indignation.

Julie sighed. 'I expect she thought it was justifiable. Emma has been naughty.'

Mrs. Hudson snorted. 'More likely she resented the fact that the lassie got so much pleasure out of it. I'm sure I hope Mr. Hillingdon will be able to talk some sense into Mr. Robert, and then we'll all have a bit of peace!'

Julie stared at her in surprise. It was the first time she had heard Mrs. Hudson get so heated about anything.

'Yes, well, I shouldn't be too optimistic,' she remarked. 'You surely know Robert well enough to realize that no one can make him do **anything**!' She walked to the door of the kitchen. 'I'd better go and see what she's doing.'

Emma was in her room, lying on her bed, staring mutinously up at the ceiling. She barely glanced at her mother as she entered the room and Julie closed the door quietly, not wanting to draw Sandra Lawson's attention to the fact that she had come to see her daughter.

'Now what's going on?' Julie began brightly. 'I hear you've been naughty again.'

Emma sniffed. 'She's cut down the swing.'

Julie sighed. 'You spilt ink all over her book.'

'No, I didn't!' Emma propped herself up on her elbows. 'I knew she'd say that, but I didn't. It was an accident.'

'Oh yes?'

'Yes. She bumped my arm and – well, the bottle turned over.'

'But what was a bottle of ink doing near your arm?'

'We were working at the table and she said for me to come round and see what she'd been doing and I went, and then – and then . . .'

'The bottle was overturned.'

'Yes.'

'I see.' Julie sighed. 'Well, I suppose she had every right to think you'd done it on purpose, hadn't she? I mean, you haven't exactly been behaving yourself, have you?'

'No, but this was different.'

'How was it different?'

'Well, I wasn't being naughty. I came round to her, just like she said, and then she bumped my arm and the ink went over her book. She was very angry with me. She said I was a disobedient little monster. Am I a disobedient little monster, Mummy?'

'Of course not, darling. Miss Lawson was just upset, that's all.'

All the same, Julie liked the sound of this less and less. It was possible that Emma was exaggerating, and surely Sandra would not be petty enough to take spite out of the child for what had happened last week-end, but even so, it was all most disturbing and distressing. She just hoped that Francis would have some success with Robert, but somehow she doubted it in the circumstances.

Looking down at Emma's indignant little face, she changed the subject. 'How about us taking a trip up to town, tomorrow? We could go and see about getting you some new clothes for the winter.'

Emma hunched her shoulders, sitting up cross-legged and resting her chin on her hands. 'Will you be able to mend the swing, Mummy?' she asked.

Julie sighed. 'Oh, I expect so.'

Emma looked up. 'Today?' Her face brightened.

'No, not today, darling.'

'When?'

'I don't know. In a few days, maybe.' Julie sighed. 'Does the idea of going up to town appeal to you?'

Emma obviously had only one thing on her mind at the moment. 'Do you think Uncle Robert will be able to mend it?' She frowned. 'I 'spect he could, don't you?'

Julie contained her impatience. This was all Robert's doing, after all. 'If he comes again,' she offered shortly. 'Now, go and wash your face and hands. It will soon be lunch time.'

During the afternoon Sandra went out, and Julie breathed a sigh of relief. The atmosphere in the house changed subtly once the governess removed her quelling presence.

Emma disappeared upstairs to her room after Sandra had left and Julie seated herself in the lounge, unconsciously waiting for the telephone to ring. She felt sure Francis would call to let her know what Robert had said.

It was a bitterly cold afternoon, but it was cosy by the fire and Julie thought she could have relaxed if only she had known that Sandra would not be returning at teatime. However, there were other problems just as disturbing to her peace of mind to torment her, and eventually she left the lounge to seek Emma's company.

But when she reached Emma's room it was empty. Frowning, Julie looked into the bathroom, but she wasn't there either. The horrible thought that she might have entered Sandra's room to wreak some awful vengeance on her property for the way she had cut down the swing that morning caused her to hasten quickly along the landing, but Sandra's room was as coldly immaculate as the woman herself.

Julie shook her head and went downstairs again. Emma must be with Mrs. Hudson.

But Mrs. Hudson was in her sitting-room and she had not seen the child. Julie felt the first twinges of anxiety. Where could she be?

'Perhaps she's in the garden,' suggested Mrs. Hudson practically.

'Oh, of course.' Julie breathed a sigh of relief. 'I didn't think of that. Not after she went upstairs earlier.'

Mrs. Hudson nodded. 'I'll come with you.'

The grey light of the afternoon shadowed the garden. A faint mist hung about the trees and the evening was drawing in, although it was scarcely half past three. It was so cold it caught Julie's breath and she shivered. It was so quiet. Surely Emma could not be out here when there was no sight nor sound of her.

'Emma!' she called, urgently. 'Emma darling! Where are you?'

There was no reply and Julie looked back at Mrs. Hudson just emerging from the house. The housekeeper looked troubled and shook her head. 'Is she not here?'

'No, I – that is – oh, *God*! is – is that her over there?'

Julie didn't wait for a reply. She was running frantically across the lawn to where the broken fibres of the swing moved slowly in the frosty air. Below their slashed threads a small body was lying, a pool of blood seeping from a head wound.

'Oh, God, Emma! Emma!' Julie was almost sobbing, bending to her knees, resting her head against the child's chilled forehead. She was scarcely conscious of Mrs. Hudson beside her, running a hand over Emma's chest, feeling for the faintly palpitating beat of a small heart.

Julie looked up at her with agonized eyes. 'Is she – is she dead?'

Mrs. Hudson shook her head, but her face like Julie's was chalk white. 'No, my love, she's not dead,' she managed, in a strained voice. 'But she's lost a lot of blood, and out here in this damp atmosphere—' She glanced round. 'Hurry into the house and call an ambulance!'

Julie hesitated, reluctant to leave her daughter, but then she realized that she was doing no good there and she sprang to her feet and ran swiftly through the hall to the lounge. Her fingers trembled violently as she tried to dial the numbers, and twice she misdialled before the sound of a car on the courtyard before the house caused her to rush to the window.

Robert was climbing out of the Aston Martin, his dark face showing little of his inner feelings. But at that moment Julie didn't particularly care what feelings he might have. Emma was hurt, badly hurt, and he might conceivably be able to help her.

She rushed through the hall again and wrenched open the door just as he reached it. One look at her face was sufficient for him to realize that something was terribly wrong.

He caught her by the forearms as she swayed slightly, and demanded: 'What's is it? In God's name, Julie, what's happened?'

In stuttering sentences, Julie managed to tell him, and he put her aside and strode through the house and into the garden, going straight to where the child lay. He looked frowningly for a moment at the broken swing and she thought he was about to question it, but then he went down on his haunches beside the unconscious child and examined the wound on her head.

'How the hell did this happen?' he asked, his voice thick with emotion.

Mrs. Hudson answered. 'From what I can see from the state of her clothes, sir, I should think she climbed the tree and fell from that branch, there. She's hit her head on the edge of the path . . . see!'

Robert nodded and rose abruptly. 'Go and get a blanket

to wrap her in, Mrs. Hudson. I'll take her in to the hospital myself.'

Mrs. Hudson looked questioningly at Julie, who nodded shakily and then the housekeeper scurried away towards the house. Julie sank down on to her knees beside Emma again, taking one of her limp little hands and cradling it in both of hers. She was choked with tears and yet they would not come. Her throat was dry and an awful sense of shock was numbing her.

Robert put his hands firmly on her shoulders and drew her to her feet. 'Don't,' he said. 'There's nothing you can do for her, and you're only upsetting yourself. Do you want to come to the hospital with me?'

'Of course.' The words were hard to articulate. She shivered and Robert drew off his sheekpskin coat and put it around her shoulders, glancing round impatiently for Mrs. Hudson. Julie tried to think. 'Is – it all right to move her?' she asked unsteadily.

Robert looked down at the small still form. 'I don't think there are any bones broken,' he said. 'And she needs to be moved from the dampness out here.'

Julie swallowed with difficulty. 'Do you – do you think she's going to be all right?'

Robert gave an ejaculation. 'Of course. Yes, of course she's going to be all right,' he replied, almost irritably, but she guessed his nerves were frayed, too.

Mrs. Hudson returned with the rug and Robert wrapped it carefully round Emma, using the utmost patience when it came to moving her injured head from the ground. Julie looked away from the seeped pool of blood. She had the awful premonition that Emma was going to die without Robert ever knowing that she was his daughter.

The journey to the hospital just outside Farnborough was a nightmare. Julie sat with Emma's head pillowed on her lap, and every now and then she removed the wad of cotton wool she had applied to the wound and replaced it with another. She was plagued with thoughts and recriminations and she could tell from Robert's grim expression that he was thoughtful, too.

At the hospital they were expected. Mrs. Hudson had phoned ahead and immediately upon arrival Emma was transferred to a stretcher trolley and wheeled away. The doctor was very kind. He showed them into a waiting-room and asked if they would remain there until Emma had been examined and her head X-rayed.

A young orderly brought them a tray of tea, but Robert wouldn't have any and Julie poured her own more out of the desire for something to do than anything else. Although Robert said little, merely inquiring whether she felt a little better now and commenting upon the coldness of the day, she was glad of his company. She was beginning to realize how dreadfully alone she would have felt had she had to come to the hospital without him.

A few minutes later, a nurse appeared in the doorway, looking rather agitatedly at Julie, who rose to her feet unsteadily.

'Mrs. Pemberton?' The nurse gestured with her arm. 'Will you come this way, please?'

Julie glanced at Robert and he nodded reassuringly. They went out of the room and along the corridor to a small examination room where Emma was still lying unconscious on the trolley.

The doctor came round to Julie as she entered. 'Ah, Mrs. Pemberton,' he said, taking her arm.

'Is something wrong?' Julie looked searchingly at Emma and then back at the doctor. 'What is it?'

'Now, now, Mrs. Pemberton, calm yourself. There's nothing wrong that we can't deal with. Emma's going to be perfectly all right, but she needs a blood transfusion.' Julie gasped and pressed a hand to her mouth as he went on:

'Unfortunately, Emma's blood group is a rather rare group, A.B. negative, in fact, and we have no blood of this grouping here. We'll have to send to one of the larger hospitals for it—'

'Robert is that blood group!' exclaimed Julie instantly, and then coloured as the doctor frowned.

'Robert?' he queried.

Julie's fingers tightened round the strap of her handbag. 'Yes – Mr. Pemberton. Emma's – that is – my brother-in-law.'

'Is he indeed?' The doctor sounded interested. 'And you think he would be prepared to be a donor—'

'Oh, I don't know – that is – perhaps,' finished Julie lamely. She half regretted telling them, but this was for Emma. Emma's life was more important than her discomfort.

Doctor Miller nodded to the nurse who had gone for Julie earlier. 'Ask Mr. Pemberton to come here,' he said, while Julie moved closer to the stretcher, looking down on Emma's waxen cheeks and blood-smeared hair compassionately. Poor little girl, she thought bitterly. And all this because of the swing. She had no doubt that Emma's intention had been to attempt to mend the swing for herself.

Robert entered the room behind the nurse, his eyes going first to Emma and then to Julie. The doctor approached him slowly, considering the notes on the pad he held in his hand. Then he looked up.

'Ah, Mr. Pemberton,' he said. 'I've just been telling Mrs. Pemberton that Emma needs a blood transfusion, but unfortunately her blood group is a rare one and therefore we're unable to perform the transfusion until blood is obtained from another hospital.'

'I see.' Robert frowned. 'And have you sent for this blood?'

'I was about to do so, Mr. Pemberton, when your – when

Mrs. Pemberton told me that you are the same rare blood group as the child.'

Robert looked taken aback. He looked quickly at Julie and then at the child. His puzzled expression revealed the way his mind was trying to assimilate what this information meant. 'You're saying, then, that I could provide the blood she needs?'

'Yes, Mr. Pemberton. If you're agreeable.'

'Of course I'm agreeable.' Robert was impatiently unbuttoning his coat, loosening the cuff of his shirt. 'Just show me what you want me to do.'

Julie was beginning to feel faint. The whole thing was too much for her to take, and she swayed unsteadily, catching the back of the chair to save herself. Doctor Miller noticed her pallor and directed the nurse who had done all the running about to take Mrs. Pemberton out of the room and find her somewhere where she could rest for a few minutes.

'Oh, but I want to stay,' began Julie urgently, a choking sensation in the back of her throat.

'There's nothing you can do,' said the nurse reassuringly. 'Come along. You don't want to be unconscious yourself when Emma recovers consciousness, do you?'

Julie cast one last appealing glance in Robert's direction, but it was impossible for her to tell what he was thinking. He was a master at disguising his thoughts, and besides, he seemed totally absorbed with what Doctor Miller was telling him.

Julie was left in the waiting-room for ages. It seemed like hours, but of course it could not have been that long. Once her head cleared, she paced the floor impatiently, eager to know what was happening, wondering where Robert was and whether he had given the blood yet. He must have done, so where was he? Had Emma been transfused?

She opened the door once and looked out on the corridor,

but apart from various orderlies and nurses dashing about seemingly intent on their own business, there was no one to advise her what was going on.

Eventually, it was the young nurse who came to find her. 'Come along, Mrs. Pemberton,' she said smilingly. 'Your daughter's recovered consciousness. Would you like to see her?'

Julie nodded speechlessly, and followed the nurse along the corridor yet again. Emma was in a side ward now, and her head had been bathed and dressed and a white bandage added to the pallor of her skin. Yet for all that she looked much better, and Julie fell on her knees beside the bed and pressed her small hand against her cheek.

'Oh, Emma!' she exclaimed, as the grey eyes flickered open, and a small smile lifted the corners of Emma's mouth.

'Hello, Mummy,' she murmured weakly. 'My head hurts.'

'I know it does, darling. You had a nasty fall. But you're going to be all right now. You're at the hospital, and everyone's been very kind.'

Emma closed her eyes and opened them again. 'I know,' she said. 'Uncle Robert told me.'

Julie glanced quickly round the room. She had been so intent on reassuring herself that Emma was recovering that she had taken little notice of the other occupants of the room. But now she saw the doctor examining his notes at the foot of the bed and the Sister who was in charge of this ward beside him. But of Robert there was no sign.

'Nurse is making Mr. Pemberton a cup of tea,' remarked the Sister at her inquiring glance. 'He thought you would prefer to see Emma alone.'

'I see.' Julie looked back at her daughter. 'Apart from your head, darling, how do you feel?'

'All right, I 'spose.' Emma frowned. 'My arm hurts and I've cut my leg.'

'All minor injuries,' said Sister, coming to the other side of the bed. 'Nothing to worry about there. And providing her head heals satisfactorily, there's no reason why she shouldn't go home in a few days.'

'A few days!' exclaimed Emma. 'But I don't want to stay here on my own.'

'You won't have to, darling,' exclaimed Julie, and looked up at the Sister. 'Can I stay? Is it possible?'

The Sister frowned. 'Well, perhaps tonight,' she agreed slowly. 'Yes, I should think we could manage that. Would you like Mummy to stay tonight, Emma?'

Emma squeezed Julie's hand. 'Oh, yes!'

'Very well, I'll go and arrange it.' The Sister walked away as Doctor Miller approached the bed.

'Well, young lady,' he said. 'I trust this will teach you the folly of climbing trees.'

Emma bit her lip. 'Did I fall out of the tree?'

'Yes, darling.' Julie got to her feet and stood looking down at her. 'But we'll talk about that later.'

'Yes, I think it's time you had a little sleep again,' said the doctor kindly. 'And don't worry. Mummy will be here when you wake up.'

Outside in the corridor again, Julie said: 'Where's Mr. Pemberton?'

'I should imagine he's back in the waiting-room again,' replied Doctor Miller. 'As you're staying, perhaps you'd like to go and explain the situation to him.'

'Y–e–s. Yes, all right.' Julie was hesitant, but she knew it had to be done.

She walked quickly back to the waiting room and pushing open the door entered the room. Robert was seated in a high-backed chair, legs apart, arms resting on his knees as he glanced casually through a magazine he had found on the table nearby. He looked up questioningly as Julie came in and she closed the door slowly and leaned back against it,

172

saying: 'They're giving her a sedative now, and she's going to sleep.'

Robert threw the magazine down and rose to his feet. 'I see.' His manner was not encouraging, and Julie hesitated before saying:

'The doctor says I can stay here tonight, and I've agreed. I wonder – would it be possible for you to drive back to the house and fetch both of us a few things? Mrs. Hudson would pack them for you.'

'Very well.' Robert inclined his head in agreement.

'She – she's much better, isn't she?'

'Much.'

'And – and it's thanks to you that she didn't have to wait for the blood to be brought here. I – I'm very grateful.'

'That's all right.' Robert glanced down momentarily. 'I'd just like to know one thing, however. How did you know that Emma and I had the same blood group?'

Julie coloured. 'Michael told me.'

'I see.' Robert's expression was grim. Then in a tortured voice, he demanded: 'For God's sake, Julie, why should Emma have my blood group and not Michael's? Only one of us had the rare grouping!'

Julie made a dismissive gesture. 'How – how should I know? These things happen—'

'Do they? Do they really?' Robert caught her by the shoulders, forcing her to look up at him. 'Julie, I want to know the truth. Is Emma my child?'

CHAPTER ELEVEN

JULIE stared at him for a long moment before speaking. She had been expecting this ever since she had so involuntarily suuplied the information about blood groups to the doctor and yet she was still unprepared for it.

'I don't think you have any right to ask such a question,' she said at last.

'Right? *Right?*' Robert was savage. 'Of course I have the right. If Emma's my daughter, I deserve to know.'

Julie tried to free herself. 'How can you say that? When you left for Venezuela without a second thought for me!'

'That's not true!' His fingers tightened, biting into her soft flesh. 'Dear God, forgive me, but my every second thought has been for you! But you married Michael, you didn't wait for me to come back, you made me despise you! And when I did return from Venezuela, I wished you dead, believe me!'

Julie quivered, trying to keep calm, but it was terribly difficult when his every touch disturbed the emotional depths of her inmost being. 'I – I wrote to you,' she stammered. 'I – I asked you to come back. I said I wanted to see you.'

'*Without giving me any reason whatsoever!*' Robert almost bit out the words. 'Just a blank statement asking me to return to England. How could I answer that? What was I supposed to make of it? Had anything changed? I *had* to go to Guaba. I had to find the cause of the explosion. How the hell could I throw everything up and return to England when all I expected from you were more recriminations, more ultimatums?' His face and voice were strained now. 'Julie, you'll never know how I felt that night when you walked out of my mother's house! You'll never know what agonies I suffered when I came to your flat and you threw my offer of marriage back in my face! I wanted you so badly, I loved you so much, that I think it was only the realization that I was needed in Guaba that kept me sane!'

Julie could not bear to meet his compelling gaze without revealing her own feelings in her eyes. 'It was all a long time ago,' she said finally.

'Not to me,' he snapped, shaking her. 'I can remember it as though it were yesterday. Do you think I haven't scourged myself with the knowledge that if I hadn't lost my temper with you, if I hadn't lost control of myself, if I hadn't behaved so – so mindlessly, that evening, you would have been prepared to see my offer for what it was: a desire to keep you with me at all costs!'

Julie moved her head slowly from side to side. 'How can I believe you?'

'God help me, it's the truth,' he groaned.

'How do I know it's not some clever ploy to induce me to confess Emma's parentage to you so that you can deprive me of my daughter completely?' Julie's voice was choked.

'*Julie!*' His thumbs moved rhythmically against the sides of her neck. 'Julie, Michael left me the responsibility for Emma. I already have the right to direct her life in whatever way I choose. Now why do you suppose he did that?'

Julie wrenched herself away, turning her back on him, hugging herself closely. 'I don't know,' she said, in a muffled voice. 'I just don't know.'

Robert uttered an imprecation. 'Of course you know, Julie. Who had a better right than I? God, Julie, say it! Tell me it's so!'

Julie swung round, her eyes wild and defensive, her lips working tremulously. 'Very well, Robert,' she cried. 'Emma is your daughter. But you'll never be able to prove it!'

Robert took a deep breath. 'So it's true,' he said, speaking in a stunned voice. 'My God!' He took a moment to take it all in. Then he said: 'Why should I want to prove it?' His eyes had narrowed and he was regarding her intently.

Julie shrugged defeatedly. 'Don't play games with me, Robert,' she said. 'I'm not a child. I know what this must mean to you. You despised me before. How much more must you despise me now? I don't suppose you consider I'm a fit and proper person to have care of *your* daughter!' Her voice broke and she turned away to hide her humiliation.

Robert made an abortive movement towards her, and then swung on his heel and left the room, leaving her standing there, her shoulders hunched, her attitude one of complete desolation.

Later that evening, an orderly brought a suitcase to the side ward where Julie was sitting with Emma. The orderly explained that the case had been left with the night porter and Julie realized that it contained the clothes she had asked Robert to collect from Mrs. Hudson.

The following morning Mrs. Hudson herself arrived to see Emma. Julie had slept little in the narrow hospital bed and was sitting with her daughter when the housekeeper arrived. The warmth of Mrs. Hudson's cheerful personality warmed Julie's chilled system, and even Emma responded to her vitality. She had brought some jigsaw puzzles and a box of felt pieces which could be pressed on to a board to make pictures, and Emma was soon engrossed.

Emma looked much better this morning, and although she never had much colour there was a definite lessening of her pallor. While she concentrated on her new toys, Mrs. Hudson looked rather reprovingly at Julie.

'What on earth happened to you last night?' she asked. 'You look terrible! All eyes. Heavens, once Mr. Robert arrived there was little chance that the child wouldn't soon be as good as new!'

Julie sighed. 'I didn't sleep very well.'

'But it's not only that, is it?' Mrs. Hudson clicked her tongue. 'Do you think I'm a fool? You're worrying about something, and Emma's illness is only part of it.' She folded her gloves. 'And as for Mr. Robert!' She raised her eyes heavenward. 'What a foul temper he was in when he came back last night! I really felt sorry for Miss Lawson.'

'Miss – Lawson?' Julie frowned at her.

'Yes, Sandra Lawson. She left this morning.'

'She did what?' Julie was astounded. 'But why?'

'Various reasons, I suppose.' Mrs. Hudson bit her lip. 'Most particularly the fact that Emma is to go to the village school, I should think.'

Julie gasped, and Emma who had apparently been engrossed in her new toys looked up in astonishment.

'Is it true?' she exclaimed excitedly. 'Mummy, is it true?'

Julie shook her head a trifle helplessly. 'If – if Mrs. Hudson says so,' she said dazedly. 'But – but why? Did he say?'

'I hardly had words with him,' replied Mrs. Hudson, enjoying her moment of importance. 'I overheard their voices in the lounge, and later Miss Lawson told me the gist of what he had said. But personally I think she kept the most of it to herself.'

'And I'm to go to school,' Emma breathed.

'It seems so,' agreed Julie. 'But – did he not mention Mr. Hillingdon?'

'Not to me, Mrs. Pemberton. As I say, he wasn't in the best of tempers when he arrived, and he hadn't improved much when he left from the sound of his tyres on the forecourt. Fair tore it up, he did.'

Julie sighed. 'Well, at least that's something we've achieved.'

Mrs. Hudson nodded. 'That's what I thought. I don't

really think Mr. Robert ever liked that woman. She wasn't the sort to have charge of a sensitive child.'

Emma bounced a little in the bed and Julie had to restrain her. 'When will I be able to start school?'

Julie drew the bedcovers straight. 'Now calm down, or you'll make your head ache again and then you'll have to stay in hospital for much longer. You'll probably start school after Christmas, when all the other children start.'

Emma clasped her hands round her drawn-up knees. 'Oh, how super!'

'Yes, but you're not to imagine you can get your own way over everything, just because in this instance, Uncle Robert—' Julie broke off. If she wasn't careful she was going to make a complete fool of herself and burst into tears.

Mrs. Hudson seemed to sense her upheaval, for she distracted Emma's attention by showing an interest in what she was doing and presently Julie got herself in control again.

Mrs. Hudson left with Julie's promise that she would ring her later in the day and let her know when she was coming home. Emma was much less tearful at the prospect of being left today and Julie thought she might go back to the house once Emma was asleep that evening.

In the afternoon they had an unexpected visitor. It was Lucy Pemberton, and she swept into the sideward like visiting royalty.

'Oh, my precious,' she exclaimed, when she saw the bandages round Emma's head. 'Darling, what have they done to you?'

Emma was not used to this kind of reaction and looked as though she was about to burst into tears, until Julie moved forward and said: 'Emma's much, much better. And the staff here have been marvellous, haven't they, darling?'

Emma nodded, but Lucy looked about her with frank distaste. 'But it's so bare!' she exclaimed. 'The child should be moved to a private nursing home, somewhere civilized, where there are carpets on the floor, and wallpaper on the walls!' Then she turned her attention back to Emma. 'Now, darling, how are you feeling?'

'I'm all right,' said Emma, looking up at Julie. She had never felt really at ease with her grandmother since the night she had been sick at Robert's apartment.

Lucy perched on the side of her bed. 'See what I've brought you,' she said, putting a parcel down in front of her. 'That's from Grandma to say what a brave little girl you've been.' Then as Emma began to unwrap the parcel she looked again at Julie. 'Why wasn't I informed of this last evening?'

Julie looked taken aback 'Were – weren't you? I – I thought that – that Robert—'

'Robert informed me this morning – by telephone,' stated Lucy disgustedly. 'Naturally he expected *you* – as her mother – to let me know.'

Julie pressed her lips together. It was obvious from Lucy's attitude that Robert had not told her about the child's parentage. But how long would it be before he did?

'I'm sorry,' she said now. 'But I shouldn't have wanted to worry you unnecessarily.'

'Unnecessarily?' Lucy drew her shoulders back. 'Julie, I'm her grandmother! I have a right to know when my granddaughter is seriously injured.'

Emma looked up from her unwrapping, her eyes wide at this piece of information.

'You're making it sound much worse than it actually was,' exclaimed Julie defensively. 'Emma was hurt, yes; she had a nasty cut on her forehead and multiple bruises, but that's all—'

'*All?* All?' Lucy was scornful. 'My dear Julie, blood transfusions are not given lightly, you know.'

Julie took a deep breath. So Robert had told his mother about the transfusion.

'What a good job there was sufficient blood on hand here to deal with it,' Lucy went on. 'Can you imagine what might have happened had they not had a supply?'

'What blood, Mummy?' Emma was looking anxious now.

'It's nothing, darling.' Julie stripped the remainder of the paper off the parcel Lucy had brought, exposing an expensively dressed doll. 'Oh, look at that! Isn't it beautiful?' She was trying to distract the child's attention, but all the while the knowledge was buzzing around in her head that Robert had not explained that he himself had been the blood donor.

Lucy was temporarily diverted by Emma's obvious pleasure in the possession of the doll, but later, when Julie escorted her along the corridor to the main entrance of the hospital, she said: 'I shall make arrangements for Emma to be transferred to the nursing home I was recommended some years ago—'.

'Please!' Julie was determined. 'I don't want her moving from here. It – it's handy for Thorpe Hulme, and I expect I shall be going back there tonight.'

Lucy was impatient. 'Then I shall speak to Robert,' she stated. 'It's inconceivable that a grandchild of mine should remain here in such awful, depressing surroundings.'

Julie shrugged. 'As you wish. I can't stop you.'

'Can't you?' Lucy shook her head. 'Robert also tells me that he has dismissed Miss Lawson.'

'So I believe.'

'Do you know why?'

'Emma is to attend the village school.'

'A *state* school!' Lucy was horrified.

'That's right.'

'Oh, but that's going too far. What can Robert be thinking of?' Her eyes narrowed. 'This is your doing, of course.'

Julie stood her ground. 'Emma needs to mix with other

children,' she said quietly. 'Surely you can see that.'

Lucy's lips twisted for a moment, and then she sighed. 'Oh, Julie,' she said, and there was a strange note of bitterness in her voice, 'I can see so much.' She took out her handkerchief and blew her nose hard. Then she looked again at her daughter-in-law, and now there was an unexpected look of pleading in her eyes. 'Julie, you won't do anything to hurt Robert again, will you?'

Julie was astounded. 'I? Hurt Robert?' she echoed.

Lucy shook her head as though to shake away her moment of appeal. 'I'm a foolish old woman,' she said shortly. 'I must go. Halbird is waiting for me. He drove me down. Good-bye, Julie.'

'Good-bye.' Julie's expression was troubled as the furcoated figure of her mother-in-law disappeared into the early evening darkness. Then she turned and went back to Emma.

Later that evening, Julie took a taxi home. The buses to Thorpe Hulme were few and far between, and besides, she was in no mood for the noise and bustle of public transport.

Mrs. Hudson welcomed her home warmly, helping her off with her coat and ushering her into the comfortable lounge. Outside it was damp and bitterly cold, but inside all was warmth and light. And yet for all that Julie felt utterly depressed.

'Have you eaten?' asked Mrs. Hudson, hovering just inside the lounge door.

Julie shook her head. 'No, but I'm not hungry—'

Then she broke off abruptly, her attention caught by an enormous vase of white roses which was standing on the table at the far side of the room. 'Where have they come from?'

Mrs. Hudson smoothed her apron. 'They arrived this afternoon, Mrs. Pemberton. Beautiful, aren't they?'

Julie frowned. 'But who are they from?'

Mrs. Hudson shrugged. 'There was no card, Mrs. Pemberton. I thought perhaps you'd know.'

Julie shook her head. 'No. No, I don't,' she said, bewilderedly. 'Have – have you heard from – from Mr. Robert today?'

'No, ma'am. Have you?'

'No. He may have rung the hospital, of course. I don't know.'

'Do you think he may have sent the roses, Mrs. Pemberton?'

Julie shook her head quickly. 'No – no, of course not. I – I just wondered if you'd heard from him.'

'I see.' Mrs. Hudson's expression portrayed her own feelings. 'And how's the little one?'

'Sleeping.' Julie sighed. 'I shall go back in the morning.'

'You look tired, ma'am. Why don't you go to bed? I could bring you up a nice warm drink of milk.'

Julie made a negative gesture. 'Not – not yet,' she answered, managing a faint smile. 'Er – where – where did Miss Lawson go?'

'Back to London I should say, madam. Although she may have gone to see Miss Hillingdon first.'

'Oh, yes, Pamela.' Julie nodded and subsided on to the couch.

'Can I get you anything?' Mrs. Hudson looked disapproving. 'You're going to make yourself ill, too, if you go on like this.'

Julie rested her head against the soft upholstery of the couch. 'I'm all right. Thank you, Mrs. Hudson.'

Suddenly on the still night air there was the sound of a car accelerating up the drive and the harsh grinding of brakes as it halted before the house. Julie was on her feet in a moment, a hasty hand smoothing the tangled disorder of her hair.

'Whoever it is I'm not in,' she said unevenly to the housekeeper. 'I – I can't face anyone now.'

'Very good, ma'am.' Mrs. Hudson went to answer the door as the bell pealed through the house, and Julie closed the lounge door behind her and leaned back against it as though she would repel any intruders by force.

However, her momentary peace was shattered by the sound of footsteps crossing the hall and the door was manually propelled open and Julie stood uncertainly to one side as Robert entered the room exuding an air of coldness and the more masculine scents of tobacco and shaving cream.

He didn't immediately see her behind the door and he looked about him with obvious impatience before he caught sight of her. Then he firmly closed the door again, and unfastened the buttons of his suede overcoat.

Julie moved away from the door, away from him, and crossed to stand on the hearth before the artificial logs of the electric fire, wishing he would say something, and when he did not, she said carefully: 'If you've come to see Emma, she's not here.'

'I know that.' Robert removed his overcoat revealing a dark lounge suit beneath. 'I've been to the hospital. I expected to find you there. I was going to bring you home. How did you get here? Did Hillingdon bring you?'

'Francis?' Julie frowned. 'No – why?'

'He said he was going to the hospital to see Emma.' He shrugged. 'It doesn't matter. It's not important.'

Julie took a trembling breath. 'You'll know that Emma is much better, then?'

'Yes. They let me see her. She was asleep, of course, but I could tell she was breathing quite naturally, and her colour was better.'

'Good. Good.' Julie was nervous and it was beginning to show.

'Damn you, aren't you going to ask me why I'm here,

183

then?' he snapped.

Julie made a helpless gesture. 'All – all right. Why are you here?'

Robert moved away from the door. In the shaded light from the lamps she could see that he looked tired, too, and there was still a look of strain around his eyes and mouth. His gaze flickered over the vase of roses on the side table and she thought he was going to make some comment about them, but instead he said: 'I came to see you, Julie.'

'Oh, yes?' Julie tugged at her ear. 'Why? I don't see what more we have to say to one another. Unless you're going to tell me when I may expect your mother to confront me with the knowledge of Emma being your daughter all along.'

'*Julie!*' His tone was tortured. 'Stop talking like that. No one will ever learn of Emma's parentage from me!'

Julie stared at him. 'How can I believe that?'

Robert shook his head slowly. 'You must think me some kind of a brute if you think I would make public the fact that my brother chose to father my child! So far as everyone else is concerned, Emma is Michael's daughter, and she'll remain that way. I could never do less for a man I loved and admired.'

Julie felt the prick of tears behind her eyes. 'I see. Then – then why did you have to know? Why did you make me tell you?'

Robert halted before her, looking down at her intently. 'Because I'm selfish enough to want to be certain that the reason you married Michael had nothing to do with falling in love with him.'

Julie trembled. 'Michael was very kind to me. I – I don't know what I should have done without him.'

'But you should have told me!' Robert exclaimed harshly. 'Julie, I was the one you should have turned to – not Michael!'

'How could I do that? You weren't there. And I could

hardly write after everything that had been said and baldly state that you would have to come home and marry me because I was pregnant? How – how charming that would have sounded!'

Robert's eyes dropped disturbingly down the length of her slender body. 'You don't seem to understand,' he said thickly. 'I would have welcomed those words from you.'

Julie's breathing felt constricted. 'How can you say that? After the way you replied to my letter.'

Robert heaved a sigh. 'I know, I know. But I was angry, don't you see? Try to understand me, Julie. You'd just refused to listen to anything I had to say. You'd refused to marry me, when I practically begged you to do so. You'd refused to understand my position with regard to the Guaba project. How was I supposed to guess the real meaning behind that stilted little letter? I tore it up. I wasn't even going to reply. But then I had second thoughts.'

Julie's nails dug into her palms. 'Why?'

Robert shook his head. 'Oh, I don't know. I suppose deep down I couldn't accept that everything was over between us. I think I half expected to see you again when I got back from Venezuela, to take up where we left off.'

'That was certainly not the impression your letter conveyed,' said Julie tautly.

'I know.' Robert raked a hand through the thickness of his dark hair, allowing his hand to rest at the back of his neck. 'I realize by replying at all I drove you to take some other means to support yourself and the child, but did you have to marry my own brother?'

Julie held up her head. 'It was no easy decision, believe me. But I was alone, and Michael was the only human being to show me a little understanding – a little kindness. He – he asked me to write to you and tell you the truth. He – he knew you would shoulder your responsibilities, but – but I didn't want you on those terms—' She moved quickly away to the other side of the room, unable to be this close to him without revealing her feelings.

But Robert moved after her, putting his hands on her hips, drawing her resisting body back against his with possessive pressure. Then she felt his mouth against the side of her neck, and his aching groan: 'Dear God, Julie, don't send me away again!'

Julie lay back against him. It was exquisite agony to feel the hardness of his body demanding a response from her. 'Robert,' she breathed protestingly, 'you may be Emma's father, but you're engaged to Pamela Hillingdon, and you've no right to make love to me like this.'

'Haven't I?' he asked huskily, twisting her round in his arms and looking deeply into her tear-drowned eyes. 'I think I have every right. I love you, Julie. I've never stopped loving you, even when I hated you, and believe me, when I found you had married Michael, I did hate you. And you love me, so don't try to deny me.'

Julie moved her head slowly from side to side. 'I – I won't deny that I love you, but I'll never be your – your mistress!'

Robert's brows drew together darkly. 'Is that what you thought I meant?' he demanded harshly. 'Is that why you – ran away from me last week-end?'

Julie shivered. 'What else could I think? As – as I've said, you're Pamela's fiancé—'

'To hell with Pamela,' he muttered savagely. 'I don't love Pamela. I never did. I told her so this morning.'

Julie blinked. 'You told her?'

'Of course. You didn't think that once I knew that you – that you hadn't stopped loving me, I could bear to share my life with any other woman?' He drew her closer so that she was intensely aware of his male strength. 'Oh, Julie, you don't know the agonies you've put me through, remembering – remembering—' His mouth sought hers gently at first and then with an increasing familiarity.

Julie clung to him weakly, her senses swimming, her body moulding itself to his almost without her will. When he finally set her free he was pale and strained.

'You've got to marry me, Julie,' he said, taking deep breaths of air into his lungs. 'Tell me you will, or God help me – I – I don't know what I'll do!'

'Oh, Robert!' Julie smoothed her hands down his cheeks, feeling the roughness of his sideburns beneath her fingers. 'I'll marry you whenever you say. But first, I – I've got to apologize, too. I was a fool six years ago. What happened was as much my fault as yours, you must know that. And – and afterwards, when I was carrying the child, it – it – oh, how can I say it?' She shook her head. 'I wanted it, can you understand that? I wanted *your* child!'

Robert pulled her close to him again, his hands in her hair, his eyes half closed and disturbingly passionate. 'You shouldn't say things like that to me right now,' he groaned. 'Because I'm wanting you very much and I've determined that I shan't touch you again until we're legally bound together.'

Julie smiled as his mouth moved across her neck, and then she said gently: 'And did you mean what you said about Emma?'

Robert looked into her face. 'Of course. Only you and I will ever know the truth of that.'

'And your mother?'

'If she's guessed, and I told her today that it was all over between Pamela and myself, she'll never say anything. That's not her way.'

'No.' Julie nodded. It also explained Lucy's rather strange and cryptic comment when she was leaving.

'Tell me something,' said Robert suddenly. 'If – if I hadn't guessed about Emma, would you have ever told me?'

Julie bent her head. 'And have you think I was trying to come between you and Pamela?'

'Hell, Julie, you must have known last week-end that what I felt for Pamela was a very paltry thing compared to my feelings for you.' He shook his head. 'Thank God Sandra cut down the swing. It's a terrible thing to say, but without Emma's accident we might have been fencing about with one another for months.'

Julie looked at him. 'You would have married Pamela in the spring.'

'You think so?' Robert shook his head again. 'From the moment you walked off the plane, from the moment I learned that Michael was dead even, I knew that sooner or later I would have to tell you how I felt.'

Julie touched his cheek. 'But that day I went out with Francis, you were so angry—'

'I was jealous!' he muttered violently. 'And if you'd had more confidence in me, you'd have seen my selfish anger for what it was.'

'Oh, Robert,' she said again, sliding her arms round his neck. Then she frowned. 'But how did you find out about the swing?'

'Mrs. Hudson told me.'

Julie smiled. 'Of course. It was lucky you were there though. It could have been so much worse. Why were you here anyway?'

Robert sighed. 'I'd been to see the Hillingdons. I'd lunched there and afterwards Francis tried to sell me some story about Emma being happier if she attended the village school.'

Julie nodded. 'I – I asked him to speak to you.'

'Yes, I know. And I was pretty mad, particularly as, after last week-end, I'd decided to give the idea a try myself.'

'Had you? Had you really?' Julie hugged him. 'Oh, darling, I'm so glad.'

'Well, it was obvious that Emma wasn't going to respond to a woman like Sandra Lawson. Besides, I didn't like the idea that she might have been placed in the household as a kind of watchdog for my misdeeds.' He smoothed her hair behind her ears. 'When will you marry me? Soon? It must be soon.'

Julie's eyes suddenly widened. 'The white roses!' she exclaimed, as everything clicked into place. 'You sent me the white roses.'

'Of course.' He nodded. 'Who else?'

Julie shook her head. 'But after yesterday evening at the hospital I hardly dared to think of you, let alone imagine you might send me flowers!'

Robert's gaze caressed her, bringing warm colour to her cheeks. 'I didn't want to leave you like that yesterday evening, but I had to speak to Pamela before I could approach you. As you said, I wasn't free, and I needed to be. I needed to be very much.'

Julie drew back a little. 'Do you — do you think the reason Michael left Emma in your care was because he hoped this might happen?' she whispered.

Robert frowned. 'Perhaps. I should think it's very possible. He knew that without some good reason you would never contact me and he needed to know that you would always be cared for.'

'But he can't have known that you — that I—'

'Can't he?' Robert shook his head. 'He must have guessed that visit he made to England when Emma was a toddler that I was more than ordinarily interested in you — in your lives out there.'

Julie allowed him to draw her closer. 'Oh, Robert,' she said, 'I'm so lucky.'

For a long moment there was an intimate silence in the lamplit lounge, but then Robert put her determinedly away from him. 'I must go,' he said rather thickly, 'or I won't go at all.'

Julie unbuttoned his jacket possessively, pressing herself against his warm body only thinly clothed in a silk shirt. 'You could use the spare bedroom now that Sandra Lawson has gone,' she suggested, but Robert shook his head.

'I somehow don't think that would work out,' he stated firmly. 'Julie, I adore you, but I've got to be sensible. Now that I know you're going to marry me, I can wait.'

Julie allowed him to fasten his jacket again and smiled. 'All right. When will I see you again?'

'I'll come for you in the morning and we'll go to the hospital and tell Emma, eh?' he murmured. 'Do you think she'll mind?'

Julie shook her head. 'She adores you, you know that.'

'And one day, when she's old enough to understand, we'll tell her the truth,' said Robert, bending to kiss Julie's cheek. 'And she will understand,' he added gently, 'because she's your daughter.'

Mills & Boon Classics

The very best of Mills & Boon romances, brought back for those of you who missed reading them when they were first published.

There are three other Classics for you to collect this January

THE SPELL OF THE ENCHANTER
by Margery Hilton
Jo needed to enlist the help of Sir Sheridan Leroy, but little did she expect that Sir Sheridan in his turn would demand *her* help to further his own personal intrigue . . .

THE LITTLE NOBODY
by Violet Winspear
Ynis had lost her memory in an accident, so she had to believe the dark and mysterious Gard St. Clair when he said that she was going to marry him . . .

MAN OUT OF REACH
by Lilian Peake
When Rosalie asked the new deputy head, Dr. Adrian Crayford, why he couldn't tolerate women, he replied that they were an irritating distraction, and the more attractive they were, the greater distraction they became. And Rosalie was attractive — and attracted to him!

If you have difficulty in obtaining any of these books from your local paperback retailer, write to:

Mills & Boon Reader Service
P.O. Box 236, Thornton Road, Croydon, Surrey, CR9 3RU

SAVE TIME, TROUBLE & MONEY!
By joining the exciting NEW...

Mills & Boon Romance CLUB

WITH all these EXCLUSIVE BENEFITS for every member

NOTHING TO PAY! MEMBERSHIP IS FREE TO REGULAR READERS!

IMAGINE the *pleasure* and *security* of having ALL your favourite *Mills & Boon* romantic fiction delivered right to *your* home, absolutely POST FREE... straight off the press! No waiting! No more disappointments! All this PLUS all the latest news of *new books* and *top-selling authors* in your own monthly MAGAZINE... PLUS *regular* big CASH SAVINGS... PLUS lots of wonderful strictly-limited, *members-only* SPECIAL OFFERS! All these exclusive benefits can be *yours* – right NOW – simply by joining the exciting NEW *Mills & Boon* ROMANCE CLUB. Complete and post the coupon below for FREE full-colour leaflet. It costs nothing. HURRY!

No obligation to join unless you wish!

FREE CLUB MAGAZINE Packed with *advance* news of latest titles and authors

Exciting offers of **FREE BOOKS** For club members ONLY

Lots of fabulous **BARGAIN OFFERS** – many at **BIG CASH SAVINGS**

FREE FULL-COLOUR LEAFLET!
CUT OUT *CUT-OUT COUPON BELOW AND POST IT TODAY!*

To: MILLS & BOON READER SERVICE, P.O. Box No 236, Thornton Road, Croydon, Surrey CR9 3RU, England.

WITHOUT OBLIGATION to join, please send me FREE details of the exciting NEW **Mills & Boon** ROMANCE CLUB and of all the exclusive benefits of membership.

Please write in BLOCK LETTERS below

NAME (Mrs/Miss) ....

ADDRESS ....

CITY/TOWN ....

COUNTY/COUNTRY .... POST/ZIP CODE ....

S. African & Rhodesian readers write to:
P.O. BOX 11190, JOHANNESBURG, 2000. S. AFRICA